contents 目錄

步驟 1

逐句跟讀電話英文關鍵句，連結你的耳和口

2 Business Calls ①
打商務電話

翻開下一頁之前，請先播放 MP3 006 ②
- ➤ 閉上眼睛聆聽內容
- ➤ 再次播放，開始進行逐句跟讀
- ➤ 專心模仿語調強弱和韻律，要與示範完全相符
- ➤ 多練習幾遍，直到能以相同速度一字不漏說出每個句子

完成逐句跟讀！請翻開下一頁，進行今天的課程 ③
- ➤ Situation 1 打電話到辦公室，找生意上的對象
- ➤ Situation 2 打電話到別家公司找客服
- ➤ 聽力練習

缺乏口型、表情、動作等視覺輔助，完全靠耳朵判斷對方所說的話，就是大家害怕用英文講電話的原因。所幸電話接通會說的就是那幾句，強迫你的耳朵和嘴巴把那些句子練到滾瓜爛熟，下次接電話即使恍神只聽到半句，也知道對方在講什麼。

① 電話單元功能

② 情境對話逐句跟讀練習

③ 課程內容主題

Situation 2
①

Calling an office to make an inquiry
MP3 008

打電話到別家公司找客服

John: Newsday Magazine. Can I help you?

Abby: Yes. I'd like to speak to someone in customer service. **②**

John: Sure. Can you hold, please?

約翰：每日新聞雜誌。有什麼可以效勞的？

艾比：嗯。我想找客服人員。

約翰：好的。請在線上等一下，好嗎？

Yes. I'd like to speak to someone in customer service.
我想找客服人員。

➡ **你也可以這樣說**

③

Yes. I need to talk to a customer service rep.
嗯。我要跟客服人員講話。

Yes. I have a customer service question.
嗯。我有一個客服相關的問題。

步驟 **2**
電話關鍵句均附多句
「你也可以這樣說」
替換，怎樣講都對！

① **主題情境對話課文**

② **電話關鍵句**

③ **關鍵句變換說法**

面對現實吧！需要學電話英文的人，就是會話能力還不足，在這種階段每通電話真正需要的，其實只有一句話。本書每通電話的關鍵句均附多句「你也可以這樣說」替換，怎樣講都對！最能提升學習信心。

如何成為電話接聽達人
使用說明

步驟 **3**

以真正的商務電話設計聽力練習，訓練聽解能力

會話能力不夠的人，「看」再多電話英文都沒用，「聽」得懂最重要！本書設計貼近辦公室電話實境的「分機表」、「行事曆」、「留言條」、「答錄機」……等練習，比照新多益聽力測驗程度出題，最符合實際商務需要。

❶ 快速解答
❷ 聽力測驗原稿

步驟 **4**

利用句子中文索引，從接通電話，到結束電話，想說的句子馬上找到

按照情境分類，想練習打電話、接電話都沒問題。書末附完整句子中文索引，臨時需要的一句話用中文查最快，一翻就找得到。

❶ 打電話關鍵句
❷ 接電話關鍵句

電話關鍵句中文索引

打電話到朋友家 **❶**

- 嗨，史帝夫在家嗎？ | Hi. Is Steve home?
- 嗨，史帝夫在家嗎？ | Hi. Is Steve around?
- 嗨，我可以跟史帝夫說話嗎？ | Hi. Can I talk to Steve?
- 嗨，我可以跟史帝夫說話嗎？ | Hi. Can I talk to Steve?
- 嗨，我是凱倫。史帝夫在家嗎？ | Hi. This is Karen. Is Steve there?
- 哈囉，皮先生。史帝夫在家嗎？ | Hello, Mr. Peters. Is Steve home?
- 嗨，抱歉這麼晚打電話來。我可以跟史帝夫說話嗎？ | Hi. Sorry for calling so late. Can I talk to Steve?
- 抱歉這麼早打擾你們，我可以跟史帝夫說話嗎？ | Hi. Sorry for disturbing you so early. Can I talk to Steve?

接聽打到公司的電話 **❷**

- 喂，泰坦保險公司，感謝您耐心等候。 | Hello. This is Titan Insurance. Thank you for waiting.
- 喂，理賠部。 | Hello. Claims Department.
- 泰坦保險公司。我是梅桓。 | Titan Insurance. Maggie speaking.
- 喂，梅桓奧柏林。 | Hello. Maggie Oberlin.
- 理賠部。我是梅桓奧柏林。 | Claims Department. This is Maggie Oberlin.
- 感謝您耐心等候。我是梅桓奧柏林。 | Thanks for waiting. I'm Maggie Oberlin.

1 Personal Calls
打私人電話

翻開下一頁之前，請先播放 **MP3 001**

➡ 閉上眼睛聆聽內容

➡ 再次播放，開始進行逐句跟讀

➡ 專心模仿語調強弱和韻律，要與示範完全相符

➡ 多練習幾遍，直到能以相同速度一字不漏說出每個句子

完成逐句跟讀！請翻開下一頁，進行今天的課程

➡ **Situation 1** 打電話到朋友家

➡ **Situation 2** 打到朋友的手機

➡ 聽力練習

Situation 1
Calling a friend at home

打電話到朋友家

Mr. Peters: Hello?

Karen: Hi. Is Steve there?

Mr. Peters: Yeah. Just a minute, I'll get him for you.

皮特先生：喂？

凱　　倫：嗨。史帝夫在嗎？

皮特先生：在。等一下，我去幫妳叫他。

Hi. Is Steve there?
嗨。史帝夫在嗎？

➡ **你也可以這樣說**

Hi. Is Steve home?
嗨。史帝夫在家嗎？

Hi. Is Steve around?
嗨。史帝夫在嗎？

Hi. Can I talk to Steve?
嗨。我可以跟史帝夫說話嗎？

Hi. Can I speak to Steve, please?
嗨。麻煩一下，我可以跟史帝夫說話嗎？

Hi. This is Karen. Is Steve there?
嗨。我是凱倫。史帝夫在嗎？

Hello, Mr. Peters. Is Steve home?
哈囉，皮特先生。史帝夫在家嗎？

Hi. Sorry for calling so late. Can I talk to Steve?
嗨。抱歉這麼晚打電話來。我可以跟史帝夫說話嗎？

Hi. Sorry for disturbing you so early. Can I talk to Steve?
抱歉這麼早打擾你們。我可以跟史帝夫說話嗎？

Situation 2
Calling a friend's cell phone
MP3 003

打電話到朋友的手機

Cathy: Hello?

Jim: Hi, Cathy?

Cathy: Yeah. What's up?

凱西：喂？

吉姆：嗨，是凱西嗎？

凱西：是啊。你好嗎？

Hi, Cathy?
嗨，是凱西嗎？

➡ **你也可以這樣說**

Hi. Is this Cathy?
嗨。凱西嗎？

Hi, Cathy. It's Jim.
嗨，凱西。我是吉姆啦。

Hi, Cathy. Can you talk now?
嗨，凱西。妳現在能講話嗎？

Hey, Cathy. Do you have a minute?
嘿，凱西。妳現在有空嗎？

Jim here. Is this a good time for you?
我是吉姆啦。妳現在方便嗎？

Hi. This is Jim. I'm a friend of Martin's.
嗨。我是吉姆。馬汀的朋友。

Hi. My name's Jim. I got your number from Martin.
嗨。我叫吉姆。我從馬汀那邊拿到妳的電話號碼。

Hi. This is Jim. Do you remember me? We met at the café last Saturday.
嗨。我是吉姆。妳記得我嗎？我們上星期六在咖啡店見過。

Listening
聽力練習 MP3 004

請聽光碟中的 3 通電話，並根據通話內容分辨來電者要找的人正在做的事，與下面哪張圖相符。

❶ _____
❷ _____
❸ _____

電話開頭必備句

MP3 005

1 Hi. Is Kevin there?

嗨。凱文在嗎？

2 Hi. Can I talk to Lisa ?

嗨。我可以跟麗莎說話嗎？

3 Hi. This is Barbara. Is Ben home?

嗨。我是芭芭拉。班恩在家嗎？

4 Hi, Josh. It's Alice.

嗨，賈許。我是愛麗斯。

5 Hi, Vicky. Can you talk now?

嗨，維琪。妳現在能說話嗎？

6 Garry here. Is this a good time for you?

我是蓋瑞。你現在方便說話嗎？

Answers & Scripts
聽力練習解答與翻譯

答案

1

A

聽力稿

W: Hello?
喂？

M: Hi. Is Nathan there?
嗨。納森在嗎？

W: It's kind of late. Could you call back tomorrow?
現在有點晚了。可以明天再打來嗎？

2

C

M: Hello?
喂？

W: Hi, Tim. This is Rhonda. Is Sally there?
嗨，提姆。我是蘭達。莎莉在家嗎？

M: Actually, she's out grocery shopping.
她正好出去買東西。

3

B

W: Hello?
喂？

M: Hi. Is Charlie home?
嗨。查理在家嗎？

W: He's out of town for the week.
他這星期到外地去玩囉。

2 Business Calls

打商務電話

翻開下一頁之前，請先播放 **MP3 006**

➡ 閉上眼睛聆聽內容

➡ 再次播放，開始進行逐句跟讀

➡ 專心模仿語調強弱和韻律，要與示範完全相符

➡ 多練習幾遍，直到能以相同速度一字不漏說出每個句子

完成逐句跟讀！請翻開下一頁，進行今天的課程

➡ **Situation 1** 打電話到辦公室找人

➡ **Situation 2** 請對方轉接客服

➡ 聽力練習

Situation 1
Calling a business associate at the office
MP3 007

打電話到辦公室找人

June: Johnson Computers. Can I help you?

Bob: Yes. I'd like to speak to Alan Rogers.

June: One moment, please.

君 ：強生電腦公司。有什麼能為您服務？

鮑伯：嗯。我要找艾倫羅傑斯。

君 ：請稍候。

Yes. I'd like to speak to Alan Rogers.
我要找艾倫羅傑斯。

➡ **你也可以這樣說**

Hello. May I speak to Alan Rogers, please?
哈囉。麻煩一下,我可以跟艾倫羅傑斯說話嗎?

Yes. I'm calling for Alan Rogers.
嗯。我要找艾倫羅傑斯。

Yes. Can you connect me with Alan Rogers, please?

嗯。請幫我轉接艾倫羅傑斯好嗎？

Hi. Can you please put me through to Alan Rogers?

嗨。可以幫我轉接艾倫羅傑斯嗎？

Hello. Can I speak to Alan Rogers in Accounting?

哈囉。我可以跟會計部的艾倫羅傑斯講話嗎？

Yes. Can you please connect me to extension 137?

嗯。可以幫我轉分機一三七嗎？

Hi. This is Bob Davis at Advanced Software. Is Alan Rogers in?

嗨。我是先進軟體公司的鮑伯戴維斯。艾倫羅傑斯在嗎？

Calling an office to make an inquiry

請對方轉接客服

John: Newsday Magazine. Can I help you?

Abby: Yes. I'd like to speak to someone in customer service.

John: Sure. Can you hold, please?

約翰：每日新聞雜誌。有什麼可以效勞的？

艾比：嗯。我想找客服人員。

約翰：好的。請在線上等一下，好嗎？

Yes. I'd like to speak to someone in customer service.
我想找客服人員。

➡ **你也可以這樣說**

Yes. I need to talk to a customer service rep.
嗯。我要跟客服人員講話。

Yes. I have a customer service question.
嗯。我有一個客服相關的問題。

Hi. Can you connect me with customer service?

嗨。可以幫我轉客服部嗎?

Could you connect me with your customer service department?

可以幫我轉貴公司的客服部嗎?

Hi. I have a question about my subscription. Can you put me though to customer service?

嗨。我有訂閱相關的問題。可以幫我轉客服部嗎?

公司部門的英文說法

- **Accounting** 會計部
- **Administration** 行政部,或稱為 Administrative
- **Advertising** 廣告部
- **Customer Service** 客服部
- **Engineering** 工程部
- **Finance** 財務部
- **Human Resources** 人事部,或稱為 Personnel
- **IT** 資訊科技部,即 information technology 的縮寫
- **Legal** 法務部

- **Logistics** 物流部
- **Manufacturing** 製造部
- **Marketing** 行銷部
- **Public Relations** 公關部,常簡稱為 PR
- **Purchasing** 採購部
- **Quality Control** 品管部,或稱為 Quality Assurance
- **R&D** 研發部,即 research and development 的縮寫
- **Sales** 業務部
- **Technical Support** 技術支援部

Listening
聽力練習 MP3 009

請聽光碟中的 3 通電話，根據通話內容分辨來電者要找下表中的哪個部門，並寫下要轉接的分機號碼。

❶ 部門：　　　　　　　　　　　　分機：

❷ 部門：　　　　　　　　　　　　分機：

❸ 部門：　　　　　　　　　　　　分機：

Departments	Extension number
Accounting	101
Human Resources	201
IT	301
Logistics	401
Marketing	501
Purchasing	601
R & D	701

電話開頭必備句

1 May I speak to Justin Smith, please?

麻煩一下，我可以跟賈斯汀史密斯講話嗎？

2 Can you connect me with May Wang, please?

請幫我轉接王美好嗎？

3 Can you please put me through to Drew Hopkins?

請幫我轉德魯霍普金好嗎？

4 Can you please connect me to extension 803?

可以幫我轉分機八〇三嗎？

5 This is Judy Chen at ABC Bank. Is Michelle Johnston in?

我是 ABC 銀行的陳茱蒂。蜜雪兒強斯頓在嗎？

6 Could you connect me with your public relations department?

可以幫我轉接貴公司的公關部嗎？

聽力練習解答與翻譯

➤ 答案

❶

部門：Human Resources Department
人事部
分機：**201**

❷

部門：**Accounting Department**
會計部
分機：**101**

❸

部門：**Purchasing Department**
採購部
分機：**601**

➤ 聽力稿

M: Global Consulting. How may I help you?
全球顧問公司。有什麼能為您效勞的？

W: Hi. I had a job interview last week, and I'm calling to see if I'm still under consideration for the position.
嗨。我上星期面試，我想打來看看我是否仍是該職位的考慮人選。

M: I see. Just a moment, please.
我瞭解了。請稍候。

W: Ralston's Office Supplies. Can I help you?
瑞斯頓辦公用品公司。有什麼能為您服務的？

M: Yes. This is Tom Jacobs with Acme Paper. We haven't received payment yet for your last printer paper order.
嗯。我是頂點紙業的湯姆傑可。我們尚未收到貴公司上個月訂購的影印紙款項。

W: OK. Can you hold for a moment?
好的。可以請您在線上稍候嗎？

M: Furniture Mart. May I help you?
這裡是家具城。有什麼可以效勞的？

W: Yes. I'm with Century Furniture. We have a new line of couches that you may be interested in selling.
嗯。我是世紀家具公司的人。我們新推出一系列沙發組，貴公司或許會有興趣銷售。

M: All right. One moment, please.
好的。請稍候。

3 How May I Help You?

有何貴幹？

翻開下一頁之前，請先播放 **MP3 011**

➡ 閉上眼睛聆聽內容

➡ 再次播放，開始進行逐句跟讀

➡ 專心模仿語調強弱和韻律，要與示範完全相符

➡ 多練習幾遍，直到能以相同速度一字不漏說出每個句子

完成逐句跟讀！請翻開下一頁，進行今天的課程

➡ **Situation 1** 接聽打來公司的電話

➡ **Situation 2** 詢問有何貴幹

➡ 聽力練習

Situation 1

Answering an office phone

MP3 012

接聽打來公司的電話

Maggie: Hello. Titan Insurance. This is Maggie speaking.

Bill: Hi. I'd like to speak to Roger Atkins, please.

Maggie: Sure. One moment.

梅姬：喂。泰坦保險公司。我是梅姬。

比爾：嗨。麻煩一下，我要找羅傑艾金斯。

梅姬：好的。請稍候。

Hello. Titan Insurance. This is Maggie speaking.
喂。泰坦保險公司。我是梅姬。

➡ **你也可以這樣說**

Hello. This is Titan Insurance. Thank you for waiting.
喂。泰坦保險公司。感謝您耐心等候。

Hello. Claims Department.
喂。理賠部。

Titan Insurance. Maggie speaking.
泰坦保險公司。我是梅姬。

Hello. Maggie Oberlin.
喂。我是梅姬奧柏林。

Claims Department. This is Maggie Oberlin.
理賠部。我是梅姬奧柏林。

Thanks for waiting. I'm Maggie Oberlin.
感謝您耐心等候。我是梅姬奧柏林。

Situation 2

Asking a caller's business

詢問有何貴幹

Zoe: [How can I help you, sir?]

Carl: I'd like to speak to Patricia Simpson in Accounting.

Zoe: [May I ask who is calling?]

柔伊：請問有何貴幹，先生？

卡爾：我要找會計部的派翠莎辛普森。

柔伊：請問是哪裡找？

How can I help you, sir?
請問有何貴幹，先生？

➡ **你也可以這樣說**

How may I help you?
請問有何貴幹？

How can I help you today?
請問有何貴幹？

What can I do for you today?
請問有何貴幹？

Who would you like to speak to/with?
請問你要找誰？

May I ask who is calling?
請問是哪裡找？

➡ **你也可以這樣說**

What is this in regard to?
請問有什麼事？

Who may I ask is calling?
請問哪裡找？

May I have your name, please?
請問貴姓大名？

Listening

聽力練習 MP3 014

請根據通話內容，在答案框補上漏寫的資訊。

For **Allan Porter**

Date **11/08/10**   Time **1:15**   A.M. **P.M.**

WHILE YOU WERE OUT

M **Ms. Cate** ▨

Of **Apex Rental**

❑ Phone **415-837-4582 ext.** ▨

❑ Fax _____

❑ Mobile _____

Area Code		Number	Extension
TELEPHONED		PLEASE CALL	×
CAME TO SEE YOU		WILL CALL AGAIN	
WANTS TO SEE YOU		URGENT	
RETURNED YOUR CALL		SPECIAL ATTENTION	

Message **Please call her back** ▨

Signed **John**

接電話開頭必備句 MP3 **015**

1 Hello. Acme Auto Parts. This is Donnie speaking.

喂。頂點汽車零件公司。我是東尼。

2 Sales Department. This is Jacob Miller.

業務部。我是雅各米勒。

3 How can I help you?

請問有何貴幹？

4 Who would you like to speak to?

請問你要找誰？

5 Who may I ask is calling?

請問哪裡找？

6 May I have your name, please?

請問貴姓大名？

Answers & Scripts
聽力練習解答與翻譯

答案

Collins
230
before 5:00 p.m. today.

聽力稿

W: Hi, may I speak to Allan Porter, please?
嗨，我可以跟艾倫波特說話嗎？

M: I'm sorry, he's out for lunch. Would you like to leave a message?
抱歉，他出去用午餐。妳要留言嗎？

W: Yes. This is Cate Collins at Apex Rental. Could you please tell him to call me back today before 5:00?
好的。我是登峰租屋的凱特柯林斯。請轉告他今天下午五點之前回電給我好嗎？

M: Sure. Can I have your number, please? And how do you spell your name?
好的。可以給我妳的電話號碼？還有妳的大名怎麼拼？

W: It's Cate with a C, Collins, C-O-L-L-I-N-S. And my number is 415-837-4582, extension 230.
C 開頭的凱特，柯林斯，C-O-L-L-I-N-S。我的電話號碼是 415-837-4582，分機 230。

4 Can I Call You Back?

我再回你電話好嗎？

翻開下一頁之前，請先播放 MP3 **016**

➡ 閉上眼睛聆聽內容

➡ 再次播放，開始進行逐句跟讀

➡ 專心模仿語調強弱和韻律，要與示範完全相符

➡ 多練習幾遍，直到能以相同速度一字不漏說出每個句子

完成逐句跟讀！請翻開下一頁，進行今天的課程

➡ **Situation 1** 告知對方你在忙，稍候回電

➡ **Situation 2** 請對方晚點再打來

➡ 聽力練習

Situation 1

Telling a caller you're busy

告知對方你在忙，稍後回電

Mark: Hi. This is Mark Jacobs. Do you have time to go over those reports?

Iris: Actually, I'm on another line. Can I call you back in 15 minutes?

Mark: Sure, no problem.

馬　克：我是馬克雅各布斯。妳有時間把那些報告看一看嗎？

艾莉斯：其實，我正在講另一通電話。我十五分鐘後回你電話好嗎？

馬　克：好的，沒問題。

I'm on another line. Can I call you back in 15 minutes?
我正在講另一通電話。我十五分鐘後回你電話嗎？

➡ **你也可以這樣說**

Sorry, I'm taking an important call. Can I call you back?
抱歉，我正在講一通重要電話。我再打給你好嗎？

I'm afraid I'm busy right now. Could I call you back later?
我現在挺忙的。我晚點再打給你好嗎？

I'm in a meeting now. Can I call when it's over?

我正在開會。開完會再打給你好嗎？

I'm driving right now, so I'll have to call you back later.

我正在開車，得晚一點再打給你了。

I'm on the train now. I'll call you when I get to the office.

我在搭地鐵／火車。我進公司會打給你。

Could I call you back from the office in about one hour?

我大約一個小時後再從公司打給你好嗎？

Situation 2

Asking a caller to call you later

請對方晚點再打來

Jeffrey: Hi, Ellen. This is Jeffrey. Are you busy?

Ellen: Well, I am in the middle of something. **Can you call back later?**

Jeffrey: Of course. It's not urgent.

傑佛瑞：嗨，愛倫。我是傑佛瑞。妳在忙嗎？

愛　倫：呃，我手上有件事正在忙。你能晚點再打來嗎？

傑佛瑞：好的。不是什麼緊急的事。

Can you call back later?
你能晚點再打來嗎？

➡ **你也可以這樣說**

Could you call back a little later?
你能晚點再打來嗎？

Could you call back in an hour?
你能過一個小時再打來嗎？

Would you mind calling back around 3 o'clock?
你介意三點左右再打來嗎？

Could you call again tomorrow?
你能明天再打來嗎？

I was just leaving for lunch. Could you call back after 1:00?
我正要去吃午餐。你能一點之後再打來嗎？

Could you call me back between 4:00 and 5:00?
你能在四點到五點間再打給我嗎？

Listening
聽力練習 MP3 019

請聽光碟中的 3 通電話，根據通話內容分辨接聽電話者應於何時打電話給誰，並在答案框上寫下該回電給誰。

❶ [　　] Call：[　　]

❷ [　　] Call：[　　]

❸ [　　] Call：[　　]

Mon Tue Wed Thu Fri Sat Sun
1 2 3 4 5 6 7
8 9 10 11 12 13 14
15 16 17 18 19 20 21
22 23 24 25 26 27 28
29 30 31

2011 2011

Mon Tue Wed Thu Fri Sat Sun
1 2 3 4 5 6 7
8 9 10 11 12 13 14
15 16 17 18 19 20 21
22 23 24 25 26 27 28
29 30 31

Today

Overnight business trip to Atlanta

Ⓐ 10:30 call [　　]

11:00 Meeting at National
        Plastics

Ⓑ 12:00 call [　　]

Tomorrow

Ⓒ 10:00 call [　　]

稍後再通電話必備句　MP3 020

1 I'm on another line. Can I call you back in half an hour?

我正在講另一通電話。我半小時後再回你電話好嗎？

2 I'm busy right now. Could I call you back later?

我在忙。我晚點再打給你好嗎？

3 I'm with a client now. Can I call you back a little later?

我正在跟客戶談事情。我晚一點再打給你好嗎？

4 I am in the middle of something. Can you call back later?

我手上有件事正在忙。你能晚點再打來嗎？

5 Could you call again on Monday?

你能星期一再打來嗎？

 答案

1

C
Roger

2

B
Rick

3

A
Pete

▶ 聽力稿

Roger: Hello, Dave. This is Roger Morton from Accounting.
喂,戴夫。我是會計部的羅傑摩頓。

Dave: Hi, Roger. I'm having lunch with clients. Is it OK if I call you back?
嗨,羅傑。我正在跟客戶吃飯。我再回電給你好嗎?

Roger: Sure. I was just wondering if those figures you promised me are ready.
好啊。我只是想知道你答應要給的那些數據準備好了沒?

Dave: Oh, right. They're in my computer at the office. Why don't I call you when I get back to the office tomorrow? I should be in by 10:00 in the morning.
哦,對。那些數據在我辦公室的電腦裡。我明天進公司再打電話給你好嗎?我早上十點應該就進公司了。

Roger: Great. I'll talk to you then.
好的。那就到時候再說囉。

Rick: Dave, this is Rick Goldberg at Allied Supplies. I've got those quotes you wanted.
戴夫,我是聯盟辦公用品的瑞克高伯格。我拿到你要的報價了。

Dave: Hi, Rick. Great. I'm in a meeting right now. Can I call you back when it's over at 12:00?
嗨,瑞克。太好了。我現在正在開會。我十二點會議結束回電話給你好嗎?

Rick: Sure, that's fine. Sorry to interrupt you.
好啊,沒問題。抱歉打擾了。

Pete: Hi, Dave. This is Pete in Marketing.
嗨,戴夫。我是行銷部的皮特。

Dave: Hi, Pete. Listen, I'm driving to a meeting. I'll get there around 10:30. Let me call you when I get there, OK?
嗨,皮特。是這樣的,我正在開車要去開會。大約十點半會到。我一到那邊就打給你,好嗎?

Pete: OK. I'll be waiting for your call.
好啊。我等你的電話。

5 Could you repeat that?

麻煩再說一遍好嗎？

翻開下一頁之前，請先播放 **MP3 021**

➡ 閉上眼睛聆聽內容

➡ 再次播放，開始進行逐句跟讀

➡ 專心模仿語調強弱和韻律，要與示範完全相符

➡ 多練習幾遍，直到能以相同速度一字不漏說出每個句子

完成逐句跟讀！請翻開下一頁，進行今天的課程

➡ Situation 1 確認來電者身分

➡ Situation 2 告知來電者你沒聽懂

➡ 聽力練習

Confirming a caller's identity

MP3
022

確認來電者身分

Paula: Can I please speak to Gary Pollard in Accounting?

John: May I have your name again, please?

Paula: Yes. I'm Paula Kirk. He's expecting my call.

寶拉：請幫我轉會計部的蓋瑞波拉德好嗎？

約翰：請問您剛剛說您貴姓大名？

寶拉：喔，我是寶拉克爾克。他知道我要打來。

May I have your name again, please?
請問您剛剛說您貴姓大名？

➡ **你也可以這樣說**

Could you repeat your name, please?
麻煩再說一次您貴姓大名？

What was your name again, please?
您剛剛說您貴姓大名？

I'm sorry. I didn't catch your name.

抱歉。我沒聽清楚您貴姓大名。

And what company are you with, Mrs. Kirk?

請問您是哪家公司，克爾克小姐？

What company do you represent, madam/sir?

小姐 / 先生，請問您代表哪家公司？

（編註：madam 為英國用語，在美國稱為 ma'am）

Could I have the name of your company again?

請再說一次您是哪間公司好嗎？

Could you please repeat your name and company?

請重複一遍您的大名和公司名稱好嗎？

Situation 2

Telling a caller you don't understand

MP3 **023**

告知來電者你沒聽懂

Gail: ATL Office Supply. How can I help you?

Barclay: Can I speak to someone in your purchasing department?

Gail: I'm sorry. I didn't catch that.

蓋　兒：ATL 辦公用品公司。有什麼可以效勞的？

巴克利：可以幫我轉採購部門的人嗎？

蓋　兒：抱歉。我沒聽清楚。

I'm sorry. I didn't catch that.
抱歉。我沒聽清楚。

➡ **你也可以這樣說**

Could you speak a little slower, please?
請講慢一點好嗎？

I'm sorry. Could you speak more clearly, please?
抱歉。請你講清楚一點好嗎？

Could you please speak a little louder?
請講大聲一點好嗎？

Sorry. I didn't understand what you said.
抱歉。我沒聽懂你剛剛說什麼。

Could you please repeat that?
請再說一遍好嗎？

Is there someone there who speaks Chinese/English?
你那裡有人會說中文 / 英文嗎？

Please hold while I get someone who speaks English.
請在線上稍候，我去找會說英文的人過來。

My English isn't very good. Could you speak slower?
我的英文不太好。你能說慢一點嗎？

Listening

聽力練習 MP3 **024**

請聽光碟中的 3 通電話，根據通話內容分辨來電者（A、B、C）。
每題對話結束後，請回答一則與通話內容相關的問題。

❶ 來電者 ⬜　　問題答案 ⬜
❷ 來電者 ⬜　　問題答案 ⬜
❸ 來電者 ⬜　　問題答案 ⬜

A

David Jackson
Branch Manager
Infinity Mortgage Co.

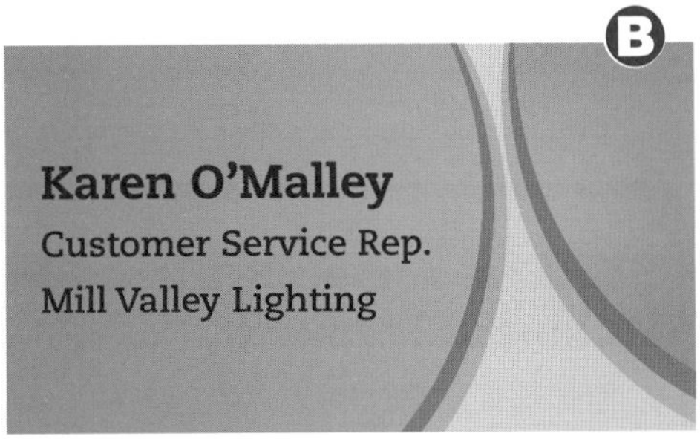

B

Karen O'Malley
Customer Service Rep.
Mill Valley Lighting

C

Bryan Lee
C.P.A.
Lee & Wilson Accounting Services

確認來電者必備句 MP3 025

1 What was your name again, please?

您剛剛說您貴姓大名？

2 Could I have the name of your company again?

請再說一次您是哪間公司好嗎？

3 Could you please repeat your name and company?

請重複一遍您的大名和公司名稱好嗎？

請對方重述必備句

1 Could you speak a little slower, please?

請講慢一點好嗎？

2 Could you please speak a little louder?

請講大聲一點好嗎？

3 Could you please repeat that?

請再說一遍好嗎？

Answers & Scripts
聽力練習解答與翻譯

▶ 答案

❶

| 來電者 B 問題答案 B |

▶ 聽力稿

W: Hi, may I speak to Mark Simmons, please? 喂，麻煩一下，可以幫我接馬克西蒙嗎？

M: I'm sorry. Mr. Simmons isn't in at the moment. May I take a message? 抱歉。西蒙先生目前不在。需要幫你留言嗎？

W: Yes. This is Karen O'Malley. I'm a customer service rep. at Mill Valley Lighting. Could you please have him call me when he returns to the office? He has my number. 好的。我是凱倫歐馬利。我是米爾谷照明燈具公司的客服代表。請他回公司後打電話給我好嗎？他有我的電話。

What is the purpose of Karen's message? 凱倫留言的目的是？

A. She wants Mr. Simmons to know that she will call him. 她要告知西蒙先生她會再來電。

B. She wants Mr. Simmons to call her when he returns. 她要西蒙先生回來時打電話給她。

C. She wants to give Mr. Simmons her phone number. 她要留電話號碼給西蒙先生。

D. She wants Mr. Simons to call her when she returns. 她要西蒙先生等她回來再打電話給她。

❷

| 來電者 C 問題答案 D |

M: Hi. Can you connect me with Paul Williams, please? 喂，請幫我轉保羅威廉斯好嗎？

W: What is this in regard to? 請問有何貴幹？

M: My name is Bryan Lee, and I'm a C.P.A. at Lee and Wilson Accounting. I had a meeting scheduled with Mr. Williams for next Tuesday, but something's come up and I want to see if we can switch to Thursday. 我是布萊恩李，李和威爾森會計事務所的會計師。我下星期二跟威廉斯先生有約，但突然有事，我想看看能不能改到星期四。

W: I see. One moment, please. I'll put you through. 好的。請等一下。我幫你轉接。

What is the purpose of Bryan's call? 布萊恩打電話的目的是？

A. He wants to schedule a meeting with Mr. Williams on Tuesday. 他想安排星期二跟威廉斯先生開會。

B. He wants to let Mr. Williams know about the new meeting time. 他要通知威廉斯先生新的開會時間。

C. He wants to cancel his Thursday meeting with Mr. Williams. 他要跟威廉斯先生取消星期四的會議。

D. He wants to reschedule his meeting with Mr. Williams. 他要跟威廉斯先生重新約開會時間。

❸

| 來電者 A 問題答案 C |

W: Allston Design Associates, Linda speaking. 艾斯頓設計事務所，我是琳達。

M: Hi. I'm David Jackson, Branch Manager at Infinity Mortgage. Is Lydia Whitman in? 妳好，我是大衛傑克森，無上限不動產抵押公司的分行經理。莉蒂亞惠門在嗎？

W: She's in a meeting right now. Would you like to leave a message? Or shall I have her call you back after the meeting? 她正在開會。你要留言嗎？還是我請她開完會之後回電給你？

M: That's all right. I'll try again tomorrow. 沒關係。我明天再打。

How will David Jackson and Lydia Whitman probably get in touch? 大衛傑克森跟莉蒂亞惠門大概會怎麼聯絡？

A. Lydia will call David back after the meeting. 莉蒂亞開完會之後會回電給大衛。

B. David will call Lydia again after the meeting. 大衛會在會議之後再打電話給莉蒂亞。

C. David will call Lydia the following day. 大衛隔天會打電話給莉蒂亞。

D. Lydia will call David back tomorrow. 莉蒂亞明天會回電給大衛。

6 We Have a bad connection.

收訊狀況很差。

翻開下一頁之前，請先播放 **MP3 026**

➡ 閉上眼睛聆聽內容

➡ 再次播放，開始進行逐句跟讀

➡ 專心模仿語調強弱和韻律，要與示範完全相符

➡ 多練習幾遍，直到能以相同速度一字不漏說出每個句子

完成逐句跟讀！請翻開下一頁，進行今天的課程

➡ **Situation 1** 告知來電者你聽不清楚

➡ **Situation 2** 請對方寄資料給你

➡ 聽力練習

Situation 1

Telling a caller you can't hear clearly

告知來電者你聽不清楚

Teresa: Hello?

Al: Hi. Teresa? This is Al. Do you have a minute?

Teresa: The reception here is really bad. I can barely hear you.
Let me call you back from a pay phone.

泰瑞莎：喂？

艾　爾：喂，泰瑞莎嗎？我是艾爾。妳有空嗎？

泰瑞莎：收訊好差。我幾乎聽不清你在說什麼。我去找個公用電話回撥
　　　　給你。

The reception here is really bad. I can barely hear you.
收訊好差。我幾乎聽不清你在說什麼。

➡ **你也可以這樣說**

**We seem to have a bad connection.
Can I call you back?**
我們似乎收訊不良。我再回電話給你好嗎？

**There's a lot of static on the line.
Can you call again?**
電話雜訊好嚴重。你能重新打電話過來嗎？

I think I'm losing you. Let me call you back.

電話快要斷訊了。我再打給你吧。

Sorry, it's really noisy here. I can't hear what you're saying.

抱歉，這裡好吵。我聽不見你說的話。

It's too noisy here. I can't hear you. Can I call you later?

這裡太吵了。我聽不見。晚點再打給你好嗎？

I can't hear you. Let me call you back from a land line.

我聽不見。我用室內電話再撥給你。

My battery's almost dead. I'll call you back from another phone.

我的電池快沒電了。我換一支電話再撥給你。

Situation 2
Requesting that information be sent
MP3 028

請對方寄資料給你

Camilla: Have you seen last month's sales chart?

Walt: No, not yet. Could you send me a copy by e-mail?

Camilla: Sure. What's your e-mail address?

卡蜜拉：你有看到上個月的銷售報表嗎？

華　特：還沒耶。可以寄一份到電子信箱給我嗎？

卡蜜拉：好啊。把你的電子郵件地址給我好嗎？

Could you send me a copy by e-mail?
可以寄一份到電子信箱給我嗎？

➡ **你也可以這樣說**

Could you e-mail me a copy of the report?
請把報告寄一份到電子信箱給我好嗎？

Can you send me a quote by e-mail or fax?
請寄到電子信箱或傳真一份報價給我好嗎？

If I give you my e-mail, could you send me the specs?

我給你我的電子郵件，你能把規格寄給我嗎？

Could you please send me the chart in an e-mail attachment?

請把圖表加在電子郵件附件寄給我好嗎？

Please e-mail the plans to me when they're ready.

計畫擬妥之後請寄電子郵件給我好嗎？

Listening
聽力練習 ^{MP3} 029

請聽光碟中的 3 通電話，並根據通話內容完成以下文件中遺漏的資訊。

1

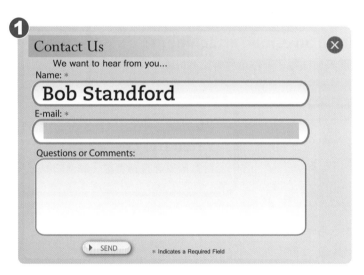

Contact Us

We want to hear from you...

Name: *

Bob Standford

E-mail: *

Questions or Comments:

▶ SEND　　* Indicates a Required Field

2

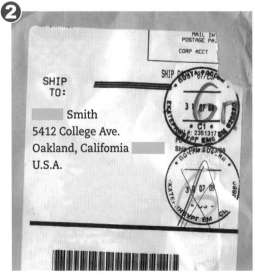

MAIL IN
POSTAGE PAI
CORP ACCT

SHIP
TO:

　　　Smith
5412 College Ave.
Oakland, California
U.S.A.

3

電話聽不清楚必備句 MP3 030

1 The reception here is really bad. I can barely hear you.

收訊好差。我根本聽不清你在說什麼。

2 There's a lot of static on the line. Can you call again?

電話雜訊好嚴重。你能重新再撥一次嗎？

3 I can't hear you. Let me call you back from a land line.

我聽不見。我用室內電話再撥給你。

4 My battery's almost dead. I'll call you back from another phone.

我的電池快沒電了。我換一支電話再撥給你。

請對方傳資料必備句

1 Could you send me a copy by e-mail or fax?

可以寄到電子信箱或傳真一份給我嗎？

2 Could you please send me the chart in an e-mail attachment?

請把圖表加在電子郵件附件寄給我好嗎？

Answers & Scripts
聽力練習解答與翻譯

答案

❶

bstanford@gmail.com

❷

Sarah
94618

❸

212-549-4477

▶ 聽力稿

M: Hi. My name is Bob Stanford. I e-mailed a question to your company through the website, but I never received an answer. So I sent the question again twice, and still no response. 喂。我是鮑伯史丹佛。我透過你們公司的網站寄了一個問題,但都沒有得到回覆。我又寄了兩次,還是沒有回音。

W: I'm sorry, Mr. Stanford. Let me look up your information. According to our records, we sent a response to you at bsanford@gmail.com. That's B-S-A-N-F-O-R-D. Is that your correct e-mail address? 抱歉,史丹佛先生。我來查一下你的資料。根據我們的紀錄,我們回覆到你的信箱 bsanford@gmail.com,B-S-A-N-F-O-R-D。這是正確的電子郵件地址嗎?

M: Actually, no. It should be B-S-T-A-N-F-O-R-D. I must have left out the "T" when I typed it in. My mistake. 其實,不是。應該是 B-S-T-A-N-F-O-R-D。我打字的時候一定是漏掉 T 了。是我的錯。

W: Not at all, sir. I'll resend our response to your correct address right away. 沒關係。我馬上把我們的回覆寄到你正確的信箱地址。

W: Hi. I'd like to order the eight gigabyte memory card in your catalog. 喂。我想要訂購你們型錄上的 8GB 記憶卡。

M: All right, ma'am. Can I have your name and address, please? 好的,小姐。請把妳的姓名及地址告訴我好嗎?

W: Sure. Sarah with an "H" Smith. My address is 5412 College Avenue, Oakland California, 94618. 好啊。有一個 H 的莎拉,史密斯。我的地址是加州奧克蘭市大學路五四一二號,區域號碼是九四六一八。

W: Hi, Robert. I hear the final draft of the contract is ready. Could you e-mail it to me? My address is rose42613@hotmail.com. 嗨,羅伯。聽說合約最後草稿已經擬好了。你可以寄電子郵件給我嗎?我的信箱地址是 rose42613@hotmail.com。

M: Actually, I don't think we have an electronic copy. Can I fax it to you? 其實,我們沒有電子檔。可以傳真給妳嗎?

W: Sure. The number is 212-549-4477. 好啊。傳真號碼是二一二 — 五四九 — 四四七七。

7

Would you like to hold?

請在線上稍候。

翻開下一頁之前，請先播放 **MP3 031**

➡ 閉上眼睛聆聽內容

➡ 再次播放，開始進行逐句跟讀

➡ 專心模仿語調強弱和韻律，要與示範完全相符

➡ 多練習幾遍，直到能以相同速度一字不漏說出每個句子

完成逐句跟讀！請翻開下一頁，進行今天的課程

➡ **Situation 1** 幫來電者轉接

➡ **Situation 2** 告知對方要找的人忙線中

➡ 聽力練習

Transferring a caller

MP3 032

幫來電者轉接

Renee: Global Medical Supplies. May I help you?

Vince: Hi. I'm calling about the sales position you have advertised.

Renee: OK, I'll transfer you to our sales department.

瑞妮：環球醫療器材公司。有什麼可以為您效勞？

文斯：嗨，我是打電話來詢問你們廣告上的業務代表工作。

瑞妮：好的，我幫你轉接到我們的業務部。

OK, I'll transfer you to our sales department.
好的，我幫你轉接到我們的業務部。

➡ **你也可以這樣說**

Please hold for a moment. I'll transfer you.
請在線上稍候。我幫你轉接。

Just a moment, I'll put you through.
請稍候，我幫你轉接。

One moment, I'll transfer you to HR.
請稍待一會兒，我幫你轉人力資源部。

Let me transfer you to the person in charge.
我幫你轉負責人。

Let me connect you with Ms. James in Sales.
我幫你轉業務部的詹姆絲小姐。

All right, let me connect you to Sales.
好的，我幫你轉業務部。

The person being called isn't available

告知對方要找的人忙線中

Sue: Sorry to keep you waiting. **Mr. Taylor is on another line right now.** Would you like to hold?

Ben: That's all right. I'll call again later.

Sue: Sure.

蘇：抱歉久等了。泰勒先生正在講另一通電話。你要在線上等嗎？

班：沒關係。我晚一點再打來。

蘇：好的。

Mr. Taylor is on another line right now.
泰勒先生正在講另一通電話。

➡ **你也可以這樣說**

His line is busy at the moment.
他現在忙線中。

He's taking another call right now.
他正在接另一通電話。

He's with a client at the moment.
他正在見一個客戶。

He's in a meeting right now.
他正在開會。

He's busy at the moment.
他正在忙。

He's not at his desk right now.
他現在不在位子上。

He's not available right now.
他現在不能聽電話。

Listening
聽力練習 MP3 034

請聽光碟中的 3 通電話，根據電話內容分辨來電者要找的人正在做的事，並從下面圖片中選出相符者。

❶ _____

❷ _____

❸ _____

Ⓐ

Ⓑ

Ⓒ

幫來電者轉接必備句 MP3 **035**

1 Please hold for a moment. I'll transfer you.
請在線上稍候。我幫你轉接。

2 Just a moment, I'll put you through.
請稍候，我幫你轉接。

轉接對象暫時無法接聽必備句

1 His line is busy at the moment.
他現在忙線中。

2 Would you like to wait?
你要在線上等嗎？

3 He's busy at the moment.
他正在忙。

4 Would you like to call back later?
你要晚點再打來嗎？

Answers & Scripts
聽力練習解答與翻譯

答案

❶

B

❷

A

❸

C

聽力稿

W: Century Software. Linda speaking.
世紀軟體公司。我是琳達。

M: Hello. Is George Hitchens in?
喂，喬治希欽斯在嗎？

W: He's out on a sales call at the moment. Would you like to leave your name and number?
他去拜訪一位客戶。你要留下姓名和電話嗎？

M: That's all right. I'll try again later.
沒關係。我晚點再打來。

M: Hi. Can you connect me with Cynthia Paulson, please?
喂。請幫我轉接辛西亞波森好嗎？

W: One moment, please…. She's not at her desk right now. Shall I have her call you back?
請稍候……。她目前不在位置上。要我請她回電給你嗎？

M: Yes, thanks. This is Tim Lee, and I'm calling about our meeting tomorrow. She has my number.
好的，謝謝。我是提姆李，我是打來跟她講明天開會的事。她有我的電話。

M: Upstate Realty. How may I help you?
上州房屋。有什麼可以為你服務？

W: I'd like to speak to Charlotte Barnes, please.
請幫我轉夏綠蒂巴恩斯。

M: Just a moment… Her line is busy now. Would you like to wait?
請稍候……。她目前忙線中。你要等嗎？

W: Actually, I'm about to leave for lunch. I'll call again in the afternoon.
其實我正要出去吃午餐。我下午再打來吧。

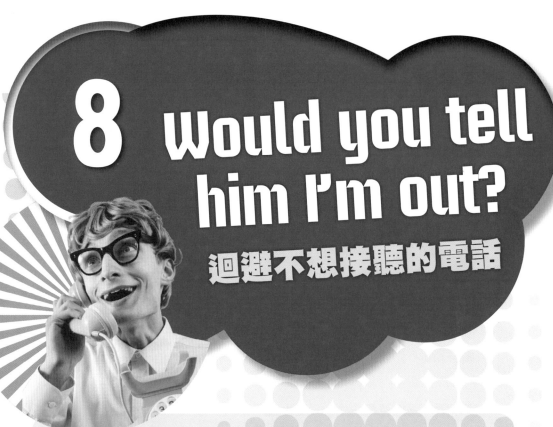

8 Would you tell him I'm out?

迴避不想接聽的電話

翻開下一頁之前，請先播放 MP3 036

➡ 閉上眼睛聆聽內容

➡ 再次播放，開始進行逐句跟讀

➡ 專心模仿語調強弱和韻律，要與示範完全相符

➡ 多練習幾遍，直到能以相同速度一字不漏說出每個句子

完成逐句跟讀！請翻開下一頁，進行今天的課程

➡ **Situation 1** 請祕書拒接電話

➡ **Situation 2** 告知對方要找的人不在

➡ 聽力練習

Declining a Phone Call

請祕書拒接電話

Sharon: Mr. Clarkson, you have a call from Ed Nelson on line four.

Mr. Clarkson: Actually, I'm a little tied up right now. Could you tell him I'll call him back?

Sharon: Sure, Mr. Clarkson. Sorry to disturb you.

莎　朗：克拉克森先生，艾德尼爾森來電，四線。

克先生：其實我現在有點忙，請跟他說我會回電好嗎？

莎　朗：好的，克拉克森先生。抱歉打擾你了。

Could you tell him I'll call him back?
請跟他說我會回電好嗎？

➡ 你也可以這樣說

Would you tell him I'm out?
跟他說我外出好嗎？

Just tell him that I'm in a meeting.
跟他說我在開會。

Could you tell him that I'm away from my desk?
請跟他說我不在座位上好嗎？

Could you get his number? I'll call him back later.
請留下他的電話號碼好嗎？我晚點回電給他。

Would you tell him I'll call him back in 30 minutes?
請跟他說我三十分鐘後回電給他好嗎？

Tell him I'll call him as soon as I get off the phone.
跟他說我一講完電話就打給他。

Situation 2
The Person Being Called Isn't In
告知對方要找的人不在

Bob: Hi. This is Bob Wright at Wilson Supplies. Can I speak to Shelly Hill, please?

Wendy: I'm afraid she's already left the office for the day.

Bob: Is there some way I could get in touch with her? It's rather urgent.

Wendy: Let me give you her cell phone number.

鮑伯：喂，我是威爾森辦公用品公司的鮑伯萊特。請幫我轉雪莉西爾好嗎？

溫蒂：她今天恐怕已經離開公司囉。

鮑伯：有能讓我聯絡到她的方法嗎？這件事很緊急。

溫蒂：我把她的手機號碼給你吧。

I'm afraid she's already left the office for the day.
她今天恐怕已經離開公司囉。

➡ 你也可以這樣說

She's not in the office right now. She should be back by 4:00.
她現在不在辦公室。四點之前應該會回來。

She stepped out for a moment. She should be back soon.
她外出一下，應該很快就會回來。

She's out to lunch. She'll be back within an hour.
她外出吃午餐，一個小時之內會回來。

She's away on business. She won't be back till Thursday.
她出差去了，要到星期四才會回來。

I'm afraid Ms. Hill is off today.
西爾小姐今天休假。

I'm afraid Ms. Hill isn't in today.
西爾小姐今天沒來。

Ms. Hill has been transferred to our London office.
西爾小姐已經轉調到倫敦辦事處。

Listening

聽力練習

MP3 039

請聽光碟中的 2 通電話，並根據通話內容回答問題。

❶

 **A** March 4th

 **B** April 3rd

 **C** March 27th

 **D** April 4th

❷

 **A** 02:00

 **B** 02:30

 **C** 03:30

 **D** 04:00

請祕書拒接電話必備句

MP3 040

1 Could you tell him I'll call him back?

請跟他說我會回電好嗎？

2 Would you tell him I'm out?

跟他說我出去了好嗎？

3 Could you get his number? I'll call him back later.

請留下他的電話號碼好嗎？我晚點回電給他。

來電要找的人不在必備句

1 She's not in the office right now.

她現在不在辦公室。

2 I'm afraid Ms. Hill isn't in today.

西爾小姐今天沒來。

3 Let me give you her cell phone number.

我把她的手機號碼給你。

Answers & Scripts
聽力練習解答與翻譯

答案

❶

D

❷

B

聽力稿

M: Hi. Can you please connect me with Craig Jensen in Marketing?
喂,請幫我轉接行銷部的克雷格詹森好嗎?

W: I'm sorry. He's out of town on business.
抱歉。他到外地出差了。

M: I see. Do you know how long he'll be gone?
了解。你知道他會去多久嗎?

W: Let's see. He left on March 27th, he's flying back on April 3rd, and he'll be back in the office on the 4th.
讓我想一下。他三月二十七日出發,四月三日的班機回來,四日會進辦公室。

What day should the man call again for Craig Jensen?
這位男士應該哪天再打電話找克雷格詹森?

A. March 4th
三月四日

B. April 3rd
四月三日

C. March 27th
三月二十七日

D. April 4th
四月四日

M: Hello. Can I speak to Carol Lopez, please?
喂,麻煩找卡蘿洛培茲好嗎?

W: Sorry, she's out on a sales call at the moment.
抱歉,她出去拜訪客戶。

M: Do you know if she'll be back soon?
她很快就會回來嗎?

W: Well, she left at 2:00 and it's 2:30 now, so she'll probably be back by 3:30 at the earliest. How about trying again at 4:00?
嗯,她兩點離開的,現在是兩點半,所以她最快大概三點半會回來。你四點再打電話來試試看好嗎?

M: Actually, it's really urgent. I'll just call her on her cell.
其實,這滿緊急的。我打她的手機好了。

When will the man probably call Carol Lopez?
這位男士可能幾點鐘會打電話給卡蘿洛培茲?

A. 2:00
兩點

B. 2:30
兩點半

C. 3:30
三點半

D. 4:00
四點

9 Is there someone else I can talk to?

轉接電話給其他人

翻開下一頁之前，請先播放 **MP3 041**

➡ 閉上眼睛聆聽內容

➡ 再次播放，開始進行逐句跟讀

➡ 專心模仿語調強弱和韻律，要與示範完全相符

➡ 多練習幾遍，直到能以相同速度一字不漏說出每個句子

完成逐句跟讀！請翻開下一頁，進行今天的課程

➡ **Situation 1** 要找的人不在，晚點再打

➡ **Situation 2** 請對方轉接電話給其他人

➡ 聽力練習

The Person You're Calling Isn't In

要找的人不在，晚點再打

Allen: Hello. Can I speak with Chuck Alston, please?

Catherine: I'm sorry. Mr. Alston isn't in now.

Allen: OK, thanks. **I'll try again later.**

艾　倫：喂，請幫我接查克艾斯頓好嗎？

凱薩琳：抱歉。艾斯頓先生不在。

艾　倫：好的，謝謝。我晚點再打。

I'll try again later.
我晚點再打。

➡ **你也可以這樣說**

I'll call again tomorrow.
我明天再打。

I'll try his cell phone.
我打他的手機。

Do you have his cell phone number?
你有他的手機號碼嗎？

Could you tell me his cell phone number? It's rather urgent.
能把他的手機號碼給我嗎？這件事很急。

Is there some way I could get in touch with him?
我有什麼方法可以跟他聯絡嗎？

When would be a good time for me to call?
我什麼時候打電話比較合適？

Do you know when he'll be back?
你知道他什麼時候會回來嗎？

When do you expect him back?
他預計什麼時候回來？

Situation 2

Asking to be Transferred to Someone Else

MP3
043

請對方轉接電話給其他人

Denise: Hi. Can I talk to George Carter in Sales?

Hugh: I'm afraid he's out on a sales call.

Denise: Oh, I see. Could you connect me with Paula Walker then?

Hugh: Sure. One moment, please.

丹妮絲： 喂，請幫我接業務部的喬治卡特好嗎？

修　　： 他出去拜訪客戶喔。

丹妮絲： 喔，這樣啊。那麼，能幫我轉接寶拉沃克嗎？

修　　： 好的。請稍候。

Could you connect me with Paula Walker then?
那能幫我轉接寶拉沃克嗎？

➡ 你也可以這樣說

Could you connect me with his supervisor then?
那麼，幫我轉接他的主管好嗎？

Could you please transfer me to someone else in Sales?
請幫我轉接業務部其他的人好嗎?

Is there someone else who could help me?
有其他人可以幫我嗎?

Is there someone else I could talk to (about…)?
有其他人可以跟我討論(這件事)嗎?

In that case, who should I speak to (about...)?
這樣的話,我該跟誰討論(這件事)?

Listening
聽力練習 MP3 044

請聽光碟中的 3 通電話，根據通話內容，配對每個人外出的理由（A、B、C、D），並寫出回來的時間。

A. on a business trip
出差

C. on vacation
去度假

B. out sick
請病假

D. at a seminar
參加研討會

1

Maggie

John

She is _____.

He is _____.

She'll be back

He'll be back

_____.

_____.

Yoko

She is   .

She'll be back on

                  .

He is   .

He'll be back

            .

Ben

Answers & Scripts
聽力練習解答與翻譯

答案

1

左：D
　　at 5:00
右：A
　　next Thursday.

2

C
on June 6th.

3

B
next week.

聽力稿

1

W: Hello. Is Maggie Coleman in?
喂，梅姬寇門在嗎？

M: I'm afraid not. She's attending a seminar, and she won't be back till 5:00.
不在喔。她去參加一個研討會，五點才會回來。

W: Oh. In that case, could you connect me with John Davis, please?
喔，這樣的話，請幫我轉接約翰戴維斯好嗎？

M: I'm sorry. He's away on business and won't be back till next Thursday.
抱歉。他出差去了，下星期四才會回來。

2

W: Hi, Samantha. This is Paul Taylor. I'm calling for Yoko.
喂，珊曼莎。我是保羅泰勒。我要找洋子。

M: Hi, Paul. Actually, Yoko's in France with her family.
嗨，保羅。其實，洋子跟她的家人去法國。

W: Wow, I'm so jealous! Do know when she'll be back?
哇，真羨慕！你知道她什麼時候回來嗎？

M: Let's see. It's May 27th, so she'll be back on the 6th of next month.
我想想看。今天是五月二十七日，她下個月六日會回來。

3

W: Hi, is this Ben?
喂，你是班嗎？

M: No, this is Steven. Ben's out with a cold.
不是，我是史蒂芬。班感冒沒來。

W: Oh, sorry to hear that. This is Christie. Do you know when he'll be back in the office?
喔，非常遺憾。我是克莉絲蒂。你知道他何時會進公司嗎？

M: Hi, Christie. I thought I recognized your voice. He was supposed to be back tomorrow, but he still has a fever, so he won't be in till next week.
嗨，克莉絲蒂。我剛剛聽聲音覺得應該是妳。他原本應該明天要進公司，但他還在發燒，所以要等到下星期了。

10 Would you like to leave a message?

你要留言嗎?

翻開下一頁之前,請先播放 **MP3 045**

➡ 閉上眼睛聆聽內容

➡ 再次播放,開始進行逐句跟讀

➡ 專心模仿語調強弱和韻律,要與示範完全相符

➡ 多練習幾遍,直到能以相同速度一字不漏說出每個句子

完成逐句跟讀!請翻開下一頁,進行今天的課程

➡ **Situation 1** 幫來電者記下留言

➡ **Situation 2** 確認人名、公司名拼法

➡ 聽力練習

Situation 1

Taking Messages

 MP3 046

幫來電者記下留言

Linda: I'm sorry, Mr. Hughes isn't in.
Would you like to leave a message?

Tom: Yes. This is Tom Adams. Could you have him call me today at 368-8525?

Linda: Sure. **Let me repeat that. Tom Adams at 368-8525, right?**

琳達：抱歉，休斯先生不在。可以請你留言嗎？

湯姆：好的。我是湯姆亞當斯。我的電話是 368-8525，可以請他今天打電話給我好嗎？

琳達：沒問題。我重複一遍。湯姆亞當斯，電話 368-8525，對嗎？

Would you like to leave a message?
可以請你留言嗎？

➡ **你也可以這樣說**

May I take a message?
需要留言嗎？

I can take a message if you'd like.
你要的話，我可以幫你留言。

May I have your name and phone number?
可以請教大名及電話嗎？

Let me repeat that. Tom Adams at 368-8525, right?
我重複一遍。湯姆亞當斯，電話 368-8525，對嗎？

➡ **你也可以這樣說**

Let me repeat your message.
我重複一次你的留言。

Let me read that back to you.
我唸一遍給你聽。

OK, that's Tom Adams at 368-8525, right?
好的，湯姆亞當斯，電話 **368-8525**，對嗎？

Tom Adams at 368-8525. Is that correct?
湯姆亞當斯，電話 **368-8525**。正確嗎？

368-8525, right?
電話 **368-8525**，對嗎？

I'm sorry. Could you repeat that number?
抱歉。你能再說一次電話號碼嗎？

Situation 2

Confirming Spellings

確認人名、公司名拼法

Billy: Ms. Parker is away from her desk. Can I take a message?

Kathy: Yes. Could you tell her that Kathy Myers at Xonar Associates called?

Billy: Certainly. **How do you spell your name, please?**

Kathy: It's Kathy with a "K," M-Y-E-R-S.

Billy: Thanks. And is that S-O-N-A-R?

Kathy: No, it's "X" as in X-ray, O-N-A-R.

比利：帕克小姐不在座位上，妳要留言嗎？

凱西：好。請跟她說索納事務所的凱西梅爾斯打電話找她好嗎？

比利：沒問題。可以請教妳的大名拼法嗎？

凱西：K 開頭的凱西，M-Y-E-R-S。

比利：謝謝。索納是 S-O-N-A-R 嗎？

凱西：不對，是 X 光的 X，O-N-A-R。

How do you spell your name, please?
可以請教妳的大名拼法嗎？

➡️ **你也可以這樣說**

Could you spell your company's name for me?
請告訴我你的公司名稱怎麼拼好嗎？

Could you please spell that for me (again)?
請（再）拼給我聽好嗎？

How do you spell your last name?
你的姓要怎麼拼？

How is your last name spelled?
你的姓要怎麼拼？

That's M-E-Y-E-R-S, right?
拼法是 M-E-Y-E-R-S，對嗎？

Is that Cathy with a "C"?
是 C 開頭的凱西嗎？

Is that "C" as in cat?
是貓那個字裡面的「 C 」嗎？

Listening 聽力練習 MP3 048

請聽光碟中的 3 通電話，並完成留言便條紙中的資訊。

1

For **Nathan Roth**

Date **11/06/27**   Time **11:00** (A.M.) P.M.

WHILE YOU WERE OUT

M **Ms.** ▓▓▓ **Smith**

Of ▓▓▓ **Consultants**

☐ Phone ▓▓▓ **8843**

☐ Fax _____

☐ Mobile _____

       Area Code   Number   Extension

TELEPHONED		PLEASE CALL	×
CAME TO SEE YOU		WILL CALL AGAIN	
WANTS TO SEE YOU		URGENT	
RETURNED YOUR CALL		SPECIAL ATTENTION	

Message **Call her when you return from** ▓▓▓

Signed **Carl**

❷

For Jane Bell

Date 11/12/14   Time 3:30   A.M. / **P.M.**

WHILE YOU WERE OUT

M Mr.

Of Boston

☐ Phone 874-8295 ext.

☐ Fax

☐ Mobile

           Area Code   Number   Extension

TELEPHONED		PLEASE CALL	
CAME TO SEE YOU		WILL CALL AGAIN	×
WANTS TO SEE YOU		URGENT	
RETURNED YOUR CALL		SPECIAL ATTENTION	

Message Will call again in the morning

           on the

Signed Zoe

❸

For Mr.

Date 11/7/6   Time   A.M. / P.M.

WHILE YOU WERE OUT

M Mr. Will

Of   Heating and cooling

☐ Phone

☐ Fax

☐ Mobile

           Area Code   Number   Extension

TELEPHONED		PLEASE CALL	×
CAME TO SEE YOU		WILL CALL AGAIN	
WANTS TO SEE YOU		URGENT	×
RETURNED YOUR CALL		SPECIAL ATTENTION	

Message Can't make appointment, wants to

           reschedule for Friday at

Signed Maggie

Answers & Scripts
聽力練習解答與翻譯

答案

1

Becky
Superior
257-8843
vacation

2

Allen Kline
Bakery
215
15th

3

Stanford
Sandburg
8 a.m.

聽力稿

1

M: Mr. Roth is away on vacation. Would you like to leave a message?
羅斯先生去度假了。妳要留言嗎？

W: Yes, please. This is Becky Smith at Superior Consulting. Could you have Nathan call me when he gets back? My number is 257-8843.
好，麻煩你了。我是優秀顧問公司的貝姬史密斯，可以請奈森回來之後打電話給我嗎？我的電話是 257-8843。

M: Is that Becky with a "Y"?
是有個 Y 的貝姬嗎？

W: Yes.
是的。

M: All right, I'll make sure Mr. Roth gets your message.
好的，我會把妳的留言轉達給羅斯先生。

2

W: I'm sorry, Ms. Bell isn't in today. Can I have your name and number?
抱歉，貝爾小姐今天不在。我可以記下你的大名和電話嗎？

M: Sure. I'm Allen Kline—that's Allen with an "E." My number is 874-8295, extension 215.
好的。我是艾倫克萊——是有 E 的艾倫，電話是 874-8295，分機 215。

W: OK. Allen K-L-I-N-E at 874-8295, right?
好。艾倫，克萊是 K-L-I-N-E，電話 874-8295，對嗎？

M: Yes, that's right. I'm with Boston Bakery. Do you know if she'll be in tomorrow?
對，沒錯。這裡是波士頓麵包店。你知道她明天會來嗎？

W: Yes, she will.
是的，她會來。

M: Great. I'll call again tomorrow morning then.
太好了。那我明天早上再打來。

3

W: Mr. Rollins is in a meeting right now. Can I take a message?
羅林斯先生正在開會。你要留言嗎？

M: Yes. This is Will Stanford at Sandburg Heating and Cooling. I have an appointment with Mr. Rollins for tomorrow at 8 a.m., but something has come up and I want to see if we can reschedule to Friday at the same time.
好。我是山伯格冷暖氣公司的威爾史丹佛。我跟羅林斯先生明天早上八點有約，但臨時有事，想看看能不能改約星期五同一時間。

W: I see. You want to reschedule from Thursday to Friday. Could you spell your company's name for me?
原來如此。你想要從星期四改到星期五。可以把公司大名拼給我嗎？

M: Yes. It's S-A-N-D-B-U-R-G. Please have him call me as soon as possible.
好的。山伯格是 S-A-N-D-B-U-R-G。請他儘快打電話給我。

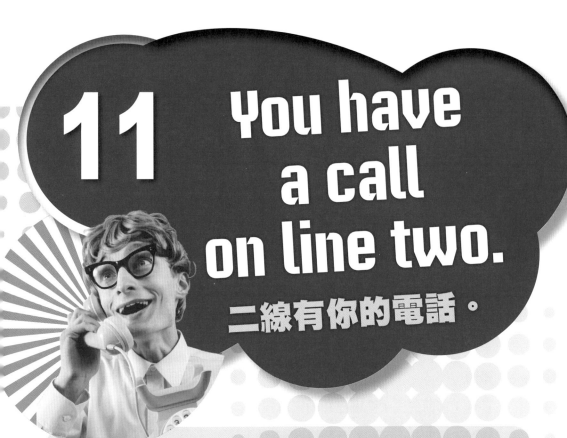

11 You have a call on line two.

二線有你的電話。

翻開下一頁之前，請先播放 **MP3 049**

➡ 閉上眼睛聆聽內容

➡ 再次播放，開始進行逐句跟讀

➡ 專心模仿語調強弱和韻律，要與示範完全相符

➡ 多練習幾遍，直到能以相同速度一字不漏說出每個句子

完成逐句跟讀！請翻開下一頁，進行今天的課程

➡ **Situation 1** 總機轉接電話

➡ **Situation 2** 部門間轉接電話

➡ 聽力練習

Situation 1

Transferring Calls (Receptionist)

總機轉接電話

Jim: Hello?

Sally: Mr. Hughes, you have a call from Susan Butler.

Jim: Thanks, Sally. Put her through.

吉姆：喂？

莎莉：修斯先生，蘇珊巴特勒來電找你。

吉姆：謝謝妳，莎莉。請轉接過來。

Mr. Hughes, you have a call from Susan Butler.
修斯先生，蘇珊巴特勒來電找你。

➡ **你也可以這樣說**

Hi, Karen. You have a call from Dale Gibson on line one.
嗨，凱倫。戴爾吉布森在一線找妳。

Robert, there's a Ms. Simpson on the line for you.
羅伯特，線上有一位辛普森小姐找你。

Mr. Webb, Mr. Porter is waiting for you on line two.

韋伯先生，波特先生在二線等你。

You have a call from Matthew Stevens at Stevens & Baker.

史蒂文貝克公司的馬修史蒂文來電找你。

There's a Bob Carter on the line. Should I put him through?

有一位鮑伯卡特在線上。要我轉接過去嗎？

MP3 **051**

Situation 2

Transferring Calls (Between Departments)

部門間轉接電話

Dan: Sales Department, Dan speaking.

Helen: Hi, Dan. This is Helen in Customer Service. I have a call for you from a customer.

Dan: OK. Thanks, Helen.

丹　：業務部，我是丹。

海倫：嗨，丹。我是客服部的海倫，有一通客戶打來的電話要找你。

丹　：好的。謝謝妳，海倫。

This is Helen in Customer Service. I have a call for you from a customer.
我是客服部的海倫，有一通客戶打來的電話要找你。

➡ **你也可以這樣說**

There's a woman on the line named Barbara Perez for you.
線上有一位叫芭芭拉裴瑞茲的女士找你。

I have a buyer from Powell Sports on the line with some questions about our new products.

我這邊有一位包威爾運動用品的採購在線上，他對我們的新產品有一些問題。

This is Adam Coleman in Sales. I have a call from Powell Sports about an invoice.

我是業務部的亞當寇門。我接到一通包威爾運動用品的電話，要問一個請款單的問題。

Mr. Jones at Powell Sports has a question about an invoice. Should I transfer him to you?

包威爾運動用品的瓊斯先生來電，他有一個關於請款單的問題。要我把他轉給你嗎？

Listening

聽力練習 MP3 052

請聽光碟中的 3 通電話，填寫出每通電話實際來電者和他想找的人。若知道想找的人是哪一個部門的，請填寫在題目後方。若無法由通話內容得知，請打叉。

A. Customer Service

B. Human Resources

C. Accounting

D. Marketing

E. Sales

Paul

Laura

Roger

Mr. Lewis

Mr. Pritchard

Jacob

Patricia

❶ The call is from _____
for _____ (in _____ Dept.).

❷ The call is from _____
for _____ (in _____ Dept.).

❸ The call is from _____
for _____ (in _____ Dept.).

Answers & Scripts
聽力練習解答與翻譯

答案

1

Jacob
Roger
C

2

Mr. Lewis
Laura
✕

3

Mr. Pritchard
Paul
E

聽力稿

M: Accounting Department, Roger speaking.
會計部，我是羅傑。

W: Hi, Roger. This is Tracy in Customer Service. I have a customer on the line who has a question about his bill. His name is Jacob Taylor.
嗨，羅傑。我是客服部的崔西。線上有一位客戶對他的帳單有疑問，他叫做雅各泰勒。

M: Thanks, Tracy. Go ahead and put him through.
謝謝妳，崔西。直接轉給我吧。

W: Hello?
喂？

M: Laura, there's a Mr. Lewis from Cohen Accounting for you on line three.
蘿拉，科恩會計公司的路易士先生找妳，在三線。

W: Did he say what it was about?
他有說要幹嘛嗎？

M: Yes. He wants to set up a time for the audit.
有的。他想要敲稽核帳目的時間。

W: Ah, right. Could you have him hold while I check my schedule, Larry?
啊，對喔。賴瑞，麻煩你請他在線上稍候，我查一下我的時間表好嗎？

M: Sales Department, this is Paul.
業務部，我是保羅。

W: Hi, Paul. There's a Mr. Pritchard for you on line two. He says he wants to place an order.
嗨，保羅。有一位皮查先生找你，在二線。他說他要下訂單。

M: Great. Thanks, Patricia.
太好了。謝謝妳，派翠夏。

12 You have an urgent call.

轉接緊急電話。

翻開下一頁之前，請先播放 **MP3 053**

➡ 閉上眼睛聆聽內容

➡ 再次播放，開始進行逐句跟讀

➡ 專心模仿語調強弱和韻律，要與示範完全相符

➡ 多練習幾遍，直到能以相同速度一字不漏說出每個句子

完成逐句跟讀！請翻開下一頁，進行今天的課程

➡ **Situation 1** 告知有緊急電話

➡ **Situation 2** 告知有私人電話

➡ 聽力練習

Situation 1

Transferring Urgent Calls

告知有緊急電話

Mr. Lewis: Hello?

Ruth: Sorry to disturb you, Mr. Lewis. **You have an urgent call from Mr. Campbell at Stockton Telecom.**

Mr. Lewis: OK, Ruth. Go ahead and put him through.

路易士先生：喂？

茹　　絲：抱歉打擾你，路易士先生。你有一通緊急電話，是史達頓電信公司的康寶先生打來的。

路易士先生：好的，茹絲。把電話轉過來吧。

You have an urgent call from Mr. Campbell at Stockton Telecom.
你有一通緊急電話，是史達頓電信公司的康寶先生打來的。

➡ **你也可以這樣說**

You have a call from Mr. Tucker at Nevada Finance. He says it's important.
你有一通電話，是內華達金融公司的塔克先生打來的。他說是要緊的事。

Sorry to interrupt. Rick Perry is on line two and he says it's an emergency.
抱歉打擾了。瑞克派瑞在二線，他說有急事。

Jack Shaw says he needs to talk to you right away. Should I put him through?
傑克蕭說他必須馬上跟你談一談。要我把電話轉給你嗎？

I know you told me to hold your calls, but the CEO is on the line for you.
我知道你說過要幫你擋電話，但執行長在線上要找你。

Situation 2
Transferring Personal Calls
告知有私人電話

Laura: James, your mom is on the line. Should I put her through?

James: Oh, no. I told her not to call me at work.

Laura: Do you want me to tell her you're busy?

James: No, I'll take it, Laura. Otherwise she'll just keep calling.

蘿　拉：詹姆士，你媽媽在線上。要我轉接給你嗎？

詹姆士：真煩。我跟她說過我上班的時候不要打給我。

蘿　拉：要我跟她說你在忙嗎？

詹姆士：不必了，我來接電話。不然她會一直打。

James, your mom is on the line.
詹姆士，你媽媽在線上。

➡ **你也可以這樣說**

You have a call from your wife, James.
你太太打電話來，詹姆士。

James, your brother is on the phone.
詹姆士，你弟弟在線上。

Your daughter is calling from London, James.
你的女兒從倫敦打電話來，詹姆士。

You have a personal call on line one.
一線有你的私人電話。

 Do you want me to tell her you're busy?
要我跟她說你在忙嗎？

➡ **你也可以這樣說**

Should I say you're in a meeting?
要我跟對方說你在開會嗎？

Shall I tell her you're away from your desk?
要我跟她說你不在位子上嗎？

I said you were busy, but she says it's urgent.
我跟她說你很忙，但她說有急事。

I can tell her you're out if you like.
如果你要的話，我可以跟她說你外出了。

Listening 聽力練習 MP3 056

請先閱讀 A-E 五樣待辦事項,再根據每題通話內容,挑出適合的待辦事項填入月曆的答案框內。

A. Pick Linda at airport **D.** Send figures to Sarah Conner

B. Meeting with Bridget Colby **E.** Repairman coming to fix air con

C. Drive Bella to piano lesson

2011 / may

Sunday	Monday	Tuesday	Wednesday	Thursday	Friday	Saturday
❶	❷	❸	❹	❺	❻	❼
❽	❾	❿ Today	⑪	⑫	⑬	⑭
⑮	⑯	⑰	⑱	⑲	⑳	㉑
㉒	㉓	㉔	㉕	㉖	㉗	㉘
㉙	㉚	㉛				

12 轉接緊急電話。

Answers & Scripts

聽力練習解答與翻譯

答案

2011 / may						
Sunday	Monday	Tuesday	Wednesday	Thursday	Friday	Saturday
①	②	③	④	⑤	⑥	⑦
⑧	⑨	**C** ⑩	⑪	**A** ⑫	⑬	⑭
⑮	⑯	⑰	⑱	⑲	⑳	㉑
㉒	**B** ㉓	㉔	㉕	㉖	㉗	㉘
㉙	㉚	㉛				

聽力稿

❶

M: Hello?
喂？

W: Hi, Stanley. This is Bridget Colby at Bridgeway Technology. Sorry to disturb you. I was just wondering if it might be possible to reschedule our meeting from next Thursday to next Friday.
嗨，史丹利。我是布吉威科技公司的布麗姬寇比。抱歉打擾你。我想問一下是否能把下週四的會議改到下週五。

M: Hmm, I'm afraid Friday isn't good for me. How about the following Monday?
嗯，下週五我恐怕不太方便。再下個星期一如何？

W: Monday is perfect. Thanks, I really appreciate it.
星期一很好。謝了，非常感謝你。

❷

M: Hi, honey.
嗨，親愛的。

W: Hi. Listen, I have to work late tonight, so do you think you could drive Bella to her piano lesson at 7:00?
嗨。我跟你說喔，我今晚必須加班，你七點能夠載貝拉去上鋼琴課嗎？

M: Sure. I'll be off by 6:00, so I'll have plenty of time.
好啊。我六點前下班，所以時間很充裕。

W: Great. Thanks, sweetie. I'll see you at home.
太好了。多謝了，親愛的。回家見。

❸

M: Hi, Linda. What's up?
嗨，琳達。還好吧？

W: Hi, Stan. It's a good thing I got hold of you. My flight's been delayed—I'll be arriving Thursday instead of tomorrow. Do you think you can pick me up?
嗨，史丹。還好我打電話找到你。我的班機延誤——我星期四才會到，明天到不了。你能開車來接我嗎？

M: I think so. What time does your flight arrive?
可以吧。妳的班機幾點抵達？

13 Please tell him to call me when he returns.

請他回來務必回電。

翻開下一頁之前，請先播放 **MP3 057**

➡ 閉上眼睛聆聽內容

➡ 再次播放，開始進行逐句跟讀

➡ 專心模仿語調強弱和韻律，要與示範完全相符

➡ 多練習幾遍，直到能以相同速度一字不漏說出每個句子

完成逐句跟讀！請翻開下一頁，進行今天的課程

➡ **Situation 1** 請對方回電

➡ **Situation 2** 請人轉告消息

➡ 聽力練習

Situation 1
Asking to have someone call you back

MP3 058

請對方回電

Bruce: Hi, this is Bruce Ellis at Farmdale Insurance. Is Mr. Lynch in?

Sherry: I'm sorry. Mr. Lynch is out at the moment. Can I take a message?

Bruce: Yes. **Can you please have him call me when he gets back? He has my number.**

布魯斯：喂，我是方戴爾保險公司的布魯斯艾力斯。林區先生在嗎？

雪　莉：抱歉。林區先生目前不在公司。需要留言嗎？

布魯斯：好的。請他回來打電話給我好嗎？他有我的電話號碼。

Can you please have him call me when he gets back? He has my number.
請他回來打電話給我好嗎？他有我的電話號碼。

➡ 你也可以這樣說

Please tell him to call me when he returns.
他回來時請他打電話給我。

Could you have him call me at my office when he gets back?

請他回來時打電話到我的公司給我好嗎？

Can you have him call me at my office? I'll be here till 6:30.

請他打電話到我的公司好嗎？我會待到六點半。

Could you please tell him to call me on my cell phone?

請他打我的手機好嗎？

Tell him to please call me as soon as possible.

請他儘快打電話給我。

Please tell him to call me at 867-5309 this afternoon.

請轉告他今天下午打 867-5309 這支電話給我。

Situation 2

Leaving a message for someone

請人轉告消息

Andy: McCarthy & Davis, how may I help you?

Dorothy: Hi. I'm Dorothy Frye at Gilroy Tool Company. May I speak to Miriam Levy, please?

Andy: I'm afraid she just stepped out. Would you like to leave a message?

Dorothy: Yes. **Please tell her I called and that I'll try again later.**

安　迪：麥卡錫戴維斯公司，有什麼可以為您效勞？

桃樂絲：喂，我是吉羅工具公司的桃樂絲弗瑞。請幫我轉蜜麗安拉維，好嗎？

安　迪：她剛剛外出一下喔。妳要留言嗎？

桃樂絲：好的。請告訴她我有來電，我晚點會再打來。

Please tell her I called and that I'll try again later.
請告訴她我有來電，我晚點會再打來。

➡ **你也可以這樣說**

Please tell her that her order is ready to pick up.
請轉告她訂的東西可以取貨了。

Tell her I sent her a fax and just wanted to confirm that she'd received it.
請轉告她，我傳真了一份文件給她，想確認她有收到。

I sent her a report by e-mail, so please tell her to check her inbox.
我寄了一份報告給她，請她查一下電子郵件信箱。

Could you let her know that I received her fax/e-mail?
請轉告她，我收到她的傳真／電子郵件了，好嗎？

Please tell her that tomorrow's meeting has been canceled.
請轉告她明天的會議取消了。

Could you tell her that the meeting's been moved from 2:30 to 3:30?
可以轉告她會議從兩點半改到三點半嗎？

Please tell her that the location of the meeting has changed. I'll e-mail her a map later.
請跟她說會議地點改了。我稍晚會用電子郵件寄地圖給她。

Listening

聽力練習 MP3 060

請聽光碟中的 2 通電話，根據通話內容完成來電者名片資料，並選出相符的來電目的。

❶

Bishop

Manager

Austin Printing

(702) 534-1182

❷

Grant Fletcher

Consultant

Sales Force

(213) 887-5485

❶ 來電目的：

A. Duane wants Don to call him back as soon as possible.

B. Dianne wants Duane to know that the manuals are ready for pick-up.

C. Duane wants to let Dianne know that he will call when the manuals are ready.

D. Duane wants Don to know that the manuals can be picked up during business hours.

❷ 來電目的：

A. Grant is calling to reschedule the seminar because he is sick.

B. Grant wants to tell Pamela that he is being replaced.

C. Grant is calling to say that he will take Drew Kinney's place.

D. Grant is calling to cancel the sales seminar.

Answers & Scripts
聽力練習解答與翻譯

▶ 答案

❶

Duane
D

❷

Consulting
B

▶ 聽力稿

W: AllTech Peripherals. This is Dianne speaking.
歐鐵克電腦周邊設備公司。我是黛安。

M: Hi, this is Duane Bishop. I'm the manager at Austin Printing. I'm calling for Don Schwartz.
嗨，我是杜安畢夏普。我是奧斯汀印刷公司的經理。我要找唐舒瓦茲。

W: He's not in today. Can I take a message?
他今天不進公司。我需要留言嗎？

M: Yes. Please tell him that the manuals have been printed and are ready for pick-up. Any time during business hours is fine, but he should call before he sends someone over. 好的。請跟他說使用手冊已經印好可以取貨了，只要是上班時間都可以來拿，但他派人來之前要先打電話通知。

What is the purpose of the call?
這通電話的目的為何？

A. Duane wants Don to call him back as soon as possible. 杜安請唐儘快回電。

B. Dianne wants Duane to know that the manuals are ready for pick-up. 黛安要通知杜安使用手冊已經可以取貨。

C. Duane wants to let Dianne know that he will call when the manuals are ready. 杜安要通知黛安等使用手冊可以取貨時，他會來電通知。

D. Duane wants Don to know that the manuals can be picked up during business hours. 杜安要通知唐上班時間可以來拿使用手冊。

W: Chantel Cosmetics. Can I help you?
香黛兒化妝品公司。有什麼可以為您效勞？

M: Yes. Can I speak to Pamela Merrill, please?
有的。可以幫我接潘蜜拉麥瑞嗎？

W: She's in a meeting right now. Can I take a message? 她正在開會。需要留言嗎？

M: Yes, thank you. I'm Grant Fletcher with Sales Force Consulting. I was supposed to lead a sales seminar at your office this afternoon at 3:00, but I've come down with a cold. I just wanted to let her know that one of our other consultants, Drew Kinney, will be taking my place. 好啊，謝謝。我是業務團隊顧問公司的格蘭特弗萊契。我原本今天下午三點要到貴公司主持一場業務座談，但我感冒了。我想通知她，另一位顧問德魯金尼會代替我去。

What is the purpose of the call?
這通電話的目的為何？

A. Grant is calling to reschedule the seminar because he is sick.
格蘭特因病來電重約座談會時間。

B. Grant wants to tell Pamela that he is being replaced. 格蘭特要通知潘蜜拉有人會代替他。

C. Grant is calling to say that he will take Drew Kinney's place. 格蘭特來電說他會代替德魯金尼。

D. Grant is calling to cancel the sales seminar.
格蘭特來電取消業務座談會。

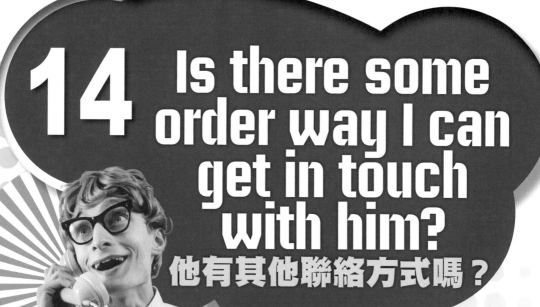

14 Is there some order way I can get in touch with him?

他有其他聯絡方式嗎？

翻開下一頁之前，請先播放 **MP3 061**

➡️ 閉上眼睛聆聽內容

➡️ 再次播放，開始進行逐句跟讀

➡️ 專心模仿語調強弱和韻律，要與示範完全相符

➡️ 多練習幾遍，直到能以相同速度一字不漏說出每個句子

完成逐句跟讀！請翻開下一頁，進行今天的課程

➡️ **Situation 1** 撥打緊急電話

➡️ **Situation 2** 首次致電給某人

➡️ 聽力練習

Situation 1
Making urgent calls

撥打緊急電話

Rosa: Hello. Can I speak to Dennis Snyder, please?

Frank: I'm sorry, ma'am. He's out of the office today.

Rosa: I have urgent business with him.
Is there some other way I can get in touch with him?

....

羅　　莎：喂。可以幫我接丹尼斯史奈德嗎？

法蘭克：抱歉，小姐。他今天不在公司。

羅　　莎：我有急事找他。有其他聯絡他的方式嗎？

I have urgent business with him.
我有急事找他。

➡ **你也可以這樣說**

I need to talk to him right away.
我必須馬上跟他談。

I need to get in touch with him immediately.
我必須立刻與他取得聯繫。

This really can't wait.
這件事很緊急。

Is there some other way I can get in touch with him?
有其他聯絡他的方式嗎？

➡ **你也可以這樣說**

Do you know how I can contact him?
你知道我該怎麼跟他聯絡嗎？

Is there another number I can reach him at?
我可以打其他電話找到他嗎？

Could you give me his cell phone number?
可以給我他的手機號碼嗎？

Calling someone for the first time

MP3 063

首次致電給某人

Doris: Riverside Automotive. How can I help you?

Walter: Hi. My name is Walter Price, and I'd like to speak to Anton Myers.

Doris: What is this regarding?

Walter: I'm with Precision Auto Parts, and I'd like to see if he may be interested in carrying our products.

桃樂絲：河濱汽車百貨。有什麼可以為您效勞？

華　特：喂。我叫華特普萊斯，我要找安東邁爾斯。

桃樂絲：請問有什麼事？

華　特：這裡是精密汽車零件公司，我想看看他是否有興趣採用我們的產品。

I'm with Precision Auto Parts, and I'd like to see if he may be interested in carrying our products.
這裡是精密汽車零件公司，我想看看他是否有興趣採用我們的產品。

➡ **你也可以這樣說**

I'm a sales rep at Johnson Supplies, and I'd like to tell him about a special offer.
我是強生辦公用品的業務代表，我想通知他一個特別優惠。

He gave me his card at a trade show and asked me to call.
他在一個商展上給我名片，要我打電話給他。

I represent a sports team, and I'd like to discuss a sponsorship deal with him.
我是一支運動隊伍的代表，我想跟他談一個贊助案。

I work for No More Hunger, and I'm wondering if he'd like to make a donation.
我服務於「不再飢餓」組織，想知道他是否願意捐款。

I'm with Metropolitan Life, and I'd like to discuss his insurance coverage.
這裡是大都會人壽，我想跟他談一下他的保險涵蓋範圍。

Listening

聽力練習

MP3
064

請聽光碟中的 3 通電話，根據通話內容分辨來電者要找的人在哪裡。

❶ ▢▢▢
❷ ▢▢▢
❸ ▢▢▢

A

B

C

Answers & Scripts
聽力練習解答與翻譯

▶ 答案

❶

B

❷

C

❸

A

▶ 聽力稿

M: Hi. Can I speak to Mark Reed, please?
喂。可以幫我接馬克瑞德嗎？

W: One moment… Sorry, he isn't answering. It's rather noisy in the shop, so he may not have heard the phone ringing.
請稍候……。抱歉，他沒接聽電話。工作坊裡很吵，他可能沒有聽到電話鈴聲。

M: It's kind of urgent—could you try again?
這件事有點急——你可以再試一次嗎？

W: Sure, no problem. I'll let it ring longer this time.
好的，沒問題。我這次會讓鈴聲響久一點。

M: Omaha Foods. Can I help you?
奧瑪哈食品公司。有什麼可以效勞的？

W: Hello. Is Joyce Cross in?
你好，喬依絲克羅斯在嗎？

M: She's at a seminar right now. She should be back by 3:00.
她在參加一個座談會。應該三點之前會回來。

W: OK, thanks. I'll call again later.
好的，多謝了。我晚一點再打來。

M: Hello. Can you please connect me with Dana Gomez?
喂。請幫我轉黛娜高梅茲好嗎？

W: Sorry, she's at the gym right now. Can I take a message?
抱歉，她現在在健身房。我可以幫你留言嗎？

M: Yes. Could you please tell her that Roy West called?
好的。請轉告她羅伊衛斯特有打電話來好嗎？

15 I call earlier, but she was out.

我稍早曾經來電，但她不在。

翻開下一頁之前，請先播放 **MP3 065**

➡ 閉上眼睛聆聽內容

➡ 再次播放，開始進行逐句跟讀

➡ 專心模仿語調強弱和韻律，要與示範完全相符

➡ 多練習幾遍，直到能以相同速度一字不漏說出每個句子

完成逐句跟讀！請翻開下一頁，進行今天的課程

➡ **Situation 1** 表明來電用意是回電

➡ **Situation 2** 再次致電

➡ 聽力練習

Returning someone's call

MP3 066

表明來電用意是回電

Abby: Ralston Brands. How can I help you?

Neal: Hi. May I speak to Nora Kerr, please?

Abby: May I ask who's calling?

Neal: This is Neal Finley at Ace Advertising.
　　　　 I'm returning her call.

愛比：瑞斯登品牌公司。有什麼可以為你效勞？

尼爾：嗨。請幫我轉諾拉柯爾好嗎？

愛比：請問是哪裡找？

尼爾：我是愛司廣告公司的尼爾芬利。我回她電話。

I'm returning her call.
我回她電話。

➡ **你也可以這樣說**

Ms. Kerr asked me to return her call.
柯爾小姐請我回電給她。

Ms. Kerr left me a message asking me to call her back.

柯爾小姐留言要我回電。

She left a message asking me to call her after 2:00.

她留言要我兩點之後回電。

I missed her call on my cell phone, so I'm calling her back.

我沒接到她打到我手機的電話，所以我回撥給她。

She called me when I was out, so I'm returning her call.

她在我外出時來電，我回她電話。

Calling someone again

MP3
067

再次致電

Julie:	Mr. Herman's office. Can I help you?
Doug:	Yes. This is Doug Crosby with Columbia Steel. I called earlier, but Mr. Herman was out.
Julie:	Ah, yes. He's expecting your call. Please hold while I put you through.

茱莉：賀門先生的辦公室。有什麼可以效勞的？

道格：妳好。我是哥倫比亞鋼鐵公司的道格克羅斯比。我稍早來電過，但賀門先生外出。

茱莉：啊，沒錯。他正在等你來電。請在線上稍候，我幫你轉接。

I called earlier, but Mr. Herman was out.
我稍早來電過，但賀門先生外出。

➡ **你也可以這樣說**

I called earlier, but the line was busy.
我稍早來電過，但電話忙線中。

I called this morning, and he asked me to call back at 2:00.

我今天早上有來電，他請我兩點再打來。

Is Mr. Herman back from lunch yet?

賀門先生用完午餐回來了嗎？

Is Mr. Herman back at his desk yet?

賀門先生回到座位了嗎？

Listening

聽力練習 MP3 068

請聽光碟中的 3 通電話，並根據通話內容選出正確的時間。

❶ _____ What time is it now?

❷ _____ When will the woman call again?

❸ _____ What time will Mr. Riley be away from the office?

Answers & Scripts
聽力練習解答與翻譯

答案

1

C

2

B

3

D

聽力稿

1

W: Copeland Foods. This is Kay speaking.
科普藍食品公司。我是凱依。

M: Hi. I'm Evan Buckley at Dover Systems. Is Norman Chan in?
嗨,我是多佛系統公司的伊凡巴克利。陳諾曼在嗎?

W: I'm afraid he's in a meeting right now.
他恐怕在開會喔。

M: I see. I called at 10:00, and he asked me to call back in an hour.
瞭解。我十點打來過,他要我過一小時再打來。

W: I'm sorry. The meeting was called at the last minute. It's scheduled to run from 10:30 to 11:30, so how about trying again at 12:00?
抱歉。這個會議是臨時通知的,預計從十點半開到十一點半,你要不要十二點打來試試看?

2

M: Hello?
喂?

W: Hi, Pete. This is Sandy. Are you ready to go over those figures with me?
嗨,皮特。我是珊蒂。你可以跟我一起看報表數字了嗎?

M: Hi, Sandy. Actually, could you call me again at 5:00?
嗨,珊蒂。事實上,妳能五點再打給我嗎?

W: But I thought you told me to call you at 3:30. I was planning on leaving office at 4:30.
但我以為你要我三點半打給你。我四點半要離開辦公室。

M: Sorry, this is taking longer than I expected. And I didn't realize you'd be leaving so early. Can you give me half an hour?
抱歉,這比我預期的還耗時間。我不知道妳那麼早就要離開。妳可以再給我半小時嗎?

W: Sure, I'll call again in half an hour.
好的,我過半小時再打給你。

3

M: Hi. Is Austin Riley in?
嗨。奧斯汀萊利在嗎?

W: He's on another line at the moment. Shall I have him call you back? 他在講另一通電話。要我請他回電嗎?

M: Actually, I was just leaving the office, and I won't be back till 2:30. I'll try again then.
其實我已經要離開辦公室,要到兩點半才會回來。我到時候再打來試試看。

W: Well, Mr. Riley will be away from his desk from 2:00 to 3:00, and he'll be out on a sales call from 3:30 to 4:30.
是這樣的,萊利先生兩點到三點不會在位子上,三點半到四點半會外出做業務拜訪。

M: OK, I guess I'll try to reach him later in the afternoon then.
好吧。看來我下午晚一點再試著找他看看吧。

16

I tried calling him, but the number was disconnected.

上次問到的聯絡方式行不通

翻開下一頁之前，請先播放 **MP3 069**

➡ 閉上眼睛聆聽內容

➡ 再次播放，開始進行逐句跟讀

➡ 專心模仿語調強弱和韻律，要與示範完全相符

➡ 多練習幾遍，直到能以相同速度一字不漏說出每個句子

完成逐句跟讀！請翻開下一頁，進行今天的課程

➡ Situation 1 再次確認聯絡方式

➡ Situation 2 打電話先寒暄幾句

➡ 聽力練習

Situation 1

Calling again when you can't get in touch with someone

再次確認聯絡方式

Helen: Tampa Group. This is Molly speaking.

Noah: Hi. This is Noah Griffin. We spoke on the phone yesterday, and I asked you for Phil Rivera's number.

Helen: Hi, Mr. Griffin. What can I do for you?

Noah: Well, I tried calling him, but the number was disconnected.

海倫：坦帕集團。我是茉莉。

諾亞：嗨，我是諾亞葛瑞芬。我們昨天通過電話，我向妳要了菲爾李維拉的電話。

海倫：嗨，葛瑞芬先生。有什麼我可以效勞的？

諾亞：是這樣的，我打過電話給他，但那個電話是空號。

I tried calling him, but the number was disconnected.
我打過電話給他，但那個電話是空號。

➡️ **你也可以這樣說**

I tried calling him, but the number is no longer in service.
我打過電話給他，但那個電話是空號。

I tried calling, but he's no longer at that number.
我打過電話給他，但那已經不是他的號碼。

I tried calling him, but I kept getting a busy signal.
我打過電話給他，但一直電話中。

The line is always busy. Do you have another number for him?
那個電話一直忙線中。妳有他的其他電話嗎？

I think I wrote the number wrong. Could you give it to me again?
我應該是抄錯電話號碼了。妳可以再給我一次嗎？

Situation 2

Making small talk

MP3 **071**

打電話先寒暄幾句

Darin: Kingston Mortgage. This is Darin speaking.

Natalie: Hi, Darin. This is Natalie Hayes at Morgan Real Estate.
How have you been lately?

Darin: Busy as usual. How about you?

Natalie: I can't complain.
If you're busy now, I can call back later.

．．．

戴　　林：金史東不動產貸款公司。我是戴林。

娜塔莉：嗨，戴林。我是摩根不動產的娜塔莉海茲。你最近還好嗎？

戴　　林：一樣很忙。妳呢？

娜塔莉：我很好。如果你正在忙，我可以晚點再打來。

How have you been lately?
你最近還好嗎？

➡ **你也可以這樣說**

How are you?
你好嗎？

How are things with you?
你都還順利吧？

How's business?
你的生意如何？

How's everything?
一切都還好吧？

If you're busy now, I can call back later.
如果你正在忙，我可以晚點再打來。

➡️ **你也可以這樣說**

Is this a good time for you?
現在打給你合適嗎？

I hope I'm not disturbing you.
希望我沒有打擾到你。

Do you have a minute?
你現在有空嗎？

Can you talk right now?
你現在方便說話嗎？

Listening

聽力練習 MP3 072

請聽光碟中的 2 通電話,並根據通話內容更正便條紙上的錯誤訊息。

❶

To: Lucy
Please call Bryan Jordan
at Silicon Industries
Tel: 432-7876

❷

To: Bret
Edith Johnson called
Conference changed to June 30th
Call her if you have questions
Tel: 854-7122

Answers & Scripts
聽力練習解答與翻譯

 答案

1

Ryan
432-7867

2

Johnston
13th
845-7122

 聽力稿

M: Hi. Can I speak to Lucy Marshall, please?
嗨，請幫我轉露西馬歇爾，好嗎？

W: I'm afraid she's away on business. Would you like to leave a message?
她出差囉。你要留言嗎？

M: Yes. This is Ryan Jordan at Silicon Industries, and my number is 432-7867. Could you please have her call me when she returns?
好。我是矽利康實業公司的萊恩喬登，我的電話是 432-7867。請她回來打電話給我好嗎？

M: Interactive Games. How can I help you?
互動遊戲公司。有什麼可以為妳效勞的？

W: Hi. Can you connect me with Bret Taylor, please?
嗨，請幫我轉布列特泰勒好嗎？

M: Mr. Taylor's meeting with a client now. Can I take a message?
泰勒先生正在跟客戶開會。妳要留言嗎？

W: Yes, please. This is Edith Johnston, and I just want to let him know that the date for the marketing conference has been rescheduled to June 13th. If he has any questions, he can reach me at 845-7122.
好的，麻煩你了。我是伊蒂絲強斯頓，我只是想通知他，行銷會議的日期已經改到六月十三日。如果他有任何疑問，請他打電話 845-7122 找我。

17 Thanks for all your help last time.

多謝你上次的大力幫忙。

翻開下一頁之前，請先播放 **MP3 073**

➡ 閉上眼睛聆聽內容

➡ 再次播放，開始進行逐句跟讀

➡ 專心模仿語調強弱和韻律，要與示範完全相符

➡ 多練習幾遍，直到能以相同速度一字不漏說出每個句子

完成逐句跟讀！請翻開下一頁，進行今天的課程

➡ **Situation 1** 打電話向對方道謝

➡ **Situation 2** 打電話向對方道歉

➡ 聽力練習

Situation 1
Small talk—thanking someone for their help

MP3 074

打電話向對方道謝

Gayle: Hi, Randy. This is Gayle Porter at Fresno Cycles.

Randy: Hi, Gayle. How are you?

Gayle: Great. I want to thank you for helping me out last time.

Randy: Sure, no problem—just doing my job.

Gayle: Well, I hope you'll let me take you out to dinner next time you're in town.

蓋麗：嗨，藍迪。我是費斯諾自行車公司的蓋麗波特。

藍迪：嗨，蓋麗。妳好嗎？

蓋麗：很好。我要謝謝你上次幫了我。

藍迪：不必客氣—只是做我該做的事。

蓋麗：嗯，希望你下次進城的時候能讓我請你去吃個晚飯。

I want to thank you for helping me out last time.
我要謝謝你上次幫了我。

➡ **你也可以這樣說**

Thanks for helping me out on that project.
上次那個案子謝謝你幫了我。

Thanks for all your help last time.
真是多謝你上次的大力幫忙。

I really appreciate all the help you've given me.
很感謝你幫我那麼多忙。

Thank you for your hospitality when I visited.
我上次去拜訪時,多謝你的招待。

Small talk—apologizing to someone

打電話向對方道歉

Kenny: Hi, June. This is Kenny Graham at Logan Glass.

June: Hi, Kenny.

Kenny: Sorry for taking so long to get back to you.

June: That's all right. I know you're busy.

Kenny: Thanks for understanding. Anyway, I have those quotes you asked for.

肯尼：嗨，君。我是羅根玻璃公司的肯尼葛拉漢。

君　：嗨，肯尼。

肯尼：抱歉拖了這麼久才回覆妳。

君　：沒關係。我知道你忙。

肯尼：謝謝妳的諒解。總之，我準備好妳要的報價了。

Sorry for taking so long to get back to you.
抱歉拖了這麼久才回覆妳。

➡️ **你也可以這樣說**

I'm sorry for taking so long to return your call.
抱歉拖了這麼久才回電。

Sorry for getting back to you so late.
抱歉這麼晚才回覆。

I'd like to apologize for the mix-up last time.
上次搞錯了真是抱歉。

Sorry again for that misunderstanding.
對於上次造成誤會，我要再說一次抱歉。

Listening
聽力練習 **MP3 076**

請聽光碟中的 3 通電話，根據通話內容在月曆上圈出正確日期。

❶

september

Sun	Mon	Tue	Wed	Thu	Fri	Sat
Today				1	2	3
4	5	6	7	8	9	10
11	(12)	13	14	15	16	17
18	19	20	21	22	23	24
25	26	27	28	29	30	

②

october

Sun	Mon	Tue	Wed	Thu	Fri	Sat
						1
2	3	4	5	6	7	8
9	10	11	12	13	14	15
16	17	18	19	20	21	22
23	24	25	26	27	28	29
30	31					

Today

③

november

Sun	Mon	Tue	Wed	Thu	Fri	Sat
		1	2	3	4	5
6	7	8	9	10	11	12
13	14	15	16	17	18	19
20	21	22	23	24	25	26
27	28	29	30			

Today

Answers & Scripts
聽力練習解答與翻譯

▶ 答案

❶

15

❷

13

❸

20

▶ 聽力稿

W: Hi, Gene?
嗨，是金嗎？

M: Speaking.
我就是。

W: This is Marina. I'm really sorry, but I don't have that estimate ready for you yet.
我是瑪莉娜。很抱歉，我還沒準備好你要的估價單。

M: That's OK. Can you send it to me by Wednesday?
沒關係。妳能在星期三之前寄給我嗎？

W: Well, I may need an extra day.
呃，我可能需要再晚一天。

M: I guess that's all right. But no later, OK?
我想應該可以吧。但不可以更晚了，好嗎？

W: Sure, no problem.
好的，沒問題。

Q: What date do Gene and Marina agree on?
金和瑪莉娜約好的日子是哪一天？

W: Tampa Storage, Adele Moran speaking.
坦帕倉儲公司，我是艾德莉莫蘭。

M: Hi, Adele. This is Kent Wong. Sorry I didn't call you when I said I would. I was really busy last week.
嗨，艾德莉。我是肯特黃。抱歉，我沒在說好的時間致電。我上星期太忙了。

W: Oh, right—you were supposed to call me that Tuesday.
喔，對耶一你原本應該星期二打給我。

M: Tuesday? I thought it was Thursday.
星期二？我以為是星期四。

W: I'm sorry, you're right.
抱歉，你是對的。

M: Hey, don't apologize—I'm the one who didn't call.
嘿，別道歉一是我沒打電話。

Q: When was Kent supposed to call Adele?
肯特原本應該哪天打電話給艾德莉？

M: Wade Caldwell, what can I do for you?
韋德卡德威，有什麼可以效勞？

W: Hi, Wade. This is Laurel.
嗨，韋德。我是蘿瑞。

M: Hey, Laurel. What's up?
嗨，蘿瑞。怎麼樣啊？

W: I'm afraid I gave you the wrong date for the marketing conference.
我告訴你的行銷會議日期恐怕是錯的。

M: You said it was on the second Monday of November, right?
妳說的是十一月的第二個星期一，對吧？

W: That's right. It's actually on the third Sunday. I gave you the date for another conference on my calendar. Sorry for the mix-up.
是啊。應該是第三個星期日才對。我把月曆上另一場會議的日期報給你了。抱歉我搞混了。

Q: What is the date of the marketing conference?
行銷會議的日期是哪一天？

18 I have someone waiting on another line.

我要接另一線電話，先講到這裡了。

翻開下一頁之前，請先播放 **MP3 077**

➡ 閉上眼睛聆聽內容

➡ 再次播放，開始進行逐句跟讀

➡ 專心模仿語調強弱和韻律，要與示範完全相符

➡ 多練習幾遍，直到能以相同速度一字不漏說出每個句子

完成逐句跟讀！請翻開下一頁，進行今天的課程

➡ **Situation 1** 指示接待人員先處理訪客

➡ **Situation 2** 要去忙別的事，結束電話

➡ 聽力練習

Situation 1

Instructing the receptionist how to handle clients when you're busy

指示接待人員先處理訪客

Mr. Harmon: Hello?

Jackie: Hi, Mr. Harmon. There's an Elliot Barber here to see you.

Mr. Harmon: Thanks, Jackie. I'm just wrapping something up. Could you tell him I'll be with him in five minutes?

Jackie: Sure, Mr. Harmon.

哈蒙先生：喂？

潔　　姬：嗨，哈蒙先生。有位艾略特巴伯來找你。

哈蒙先生：謝謝，潔姬。我手上的事正要處理完。請告訴他我五分鐘後去找他，好嗎？

潔　　姬：好的，哈蒙先生。

Could you tell him I'll be with him in five minutes?
請告訴他我五分鐘後去找他，好嗎？

➡ **你也可以這樣說**

Please tell him I'll be with him shortly.
請告訴他我過一下就去找他。

Could you ask him to have a seat?
請他坐一下，好嗎？

Could you please take him to the conference room?
請帶他去會議室，好嗎？

Could you have him wait in the conference room?
請他在會議室等一下，好嗎？

Could you ask Tom Estrada to go out and greet him?
請找湯姆艾斯特拉達出去接待他，好嗎？

Situation 2
Ending a call when you're busy 🎵 **079**

要去忙別的事，結束電話

Trent: Also, I have a few questions about billing. Could you help me?

Holly: I'm sorry. I have someone waiting on another line. I can call you back if you like.

Trent: OK. That would be fine.

川特：此外，我還有幾個關於帳單的問題。妳能幫我嗎？

荷莉：抱歉。我要接另一線電話。如果你要的話，我可以再打給你。

川特：好的。沒問題。

I have someone waiting on another line.
我要接另一線電話。

➡ 你也可以這樣說

I'm a little busy at the moment.
我現在有點忙。

I was just leaving.
我已經要離開了。

I'm with a client.
我和客戶在談事情。

I'm afraid I can't help you with that.
這件事我恐怕幫不上忙。

I can call you back if you like.
如果你要的話，我可以再打給你。

➡️ **你也可以這樣說**

Could you call back later?
你可以晚點再打來嗎？

I'll have to get back to you on that.
我得晚點再打給你講這件事了。

Let me connect you with someone else.
我幫你把電話轉給另一個人。

If you leave your number, I can have someone get back to you.
如果你留下電話號碼，我可以請人回電給你。

Listening
聽力練習 MP3 080

請聽 3 通電話，判斷接待人員要將訪客帶到哪一個地點。

❶
❷
❸

A

B

C

Answers & Scripts
聽力練習解答與翻譯

答案

①

C

②

B

③

A

聽力稿

①

W: Hi, Mr. Blake. Anton Vargas from the L.A. office is here in the lobby. Should I send him up to your office?
嗨，布萊克先生。洛杉磯分公司的安東瓦格斯來到大廳了。我該讓他上樓去你的辦公室嗎？

M: Actually, we're meeting for lunch in the employee lounge. Could you show him where it is?
其實，我們要在員工休息區碰面一起用午餐。請妳告訴他怎麼走，好嗎？

W: Sure, Mr. Blake.
好的，布萊克先生。

②

M: Hi, Alice. Lynn McGee is here to see you.
嗨，愛麗斯。琳恩麥基來找妳。

W: Thanks, Robbie. Could you take her to the conference room for me? I'll be there shortly.
謝謝你，羅比。請幫我帶她到會議室好嗎？我很快就過去。

M: Sure, Alice. No problem.
好的，愛麗斯。沒問題。

③

W: Mr. Ingram, are you expecting a Mr. Tate?
英格先生，你有約一位泰德先生嗎？

M: Yes. We have a two o'clock appointment. Is he here already?
有。我們兩點有約。他已經到了嗎？

W: Yes. He's here at the reception desk.
對，他在接待櫃臺這邊。

M: OK. I'm still in a meeting here. Could you have him wait in my office?
好，我還在開會。請讓他在我的辦公室等候，好嗎？

19 One more thing before we hang up....

掛電話前再提醒一下……

翻開下一頁之前，請先播放 **MP3 081**

➡ 閉上眼睛聆聽內容

➡ 再次播放，開始進行逐句跟讀

➡ 專心模仿語調強弱和韻律，要與示範完全相符

➡ 多練習幾遍，直到能以相同速度一字不漏說出每個句子

完成逐句跟讀！請翻開下一頁，進行今天的課程

➡ **Situation 1** 結束電話前的提醒

➡ **Situation 2** 對方忙碌時，結束電話

➡ 聽力練習

Situation 1

Ending a call with a reminder

MP3 082

結束電話前的提醒

Neal: Well, we should get back to work. I'll talk to you later, Paula.

Paula: OK. Oh, right. One more thing before we hang up....

Neal: Yeah?

Paula: Don't forget about the dinner next Friday.

Neal: OK, I won't. Bye now.

尼爾：嗯，我們該回去工作了。晚點再聊囉，寶拉。

寶拉：好。喔，對了。掛電話前還有一件事提醒一下……。

尼爾：什麼？

寶拉：別忘了下星期五要一起吃晚餐。

尼爾：好的，我不會忘記。那就再見囉。

One more thing before we hang up....
掛電話前還有一件事提醒一下……。

➡ 你也可以這樣說

While I still have you on the line....
趁你還在線上……。

In case I don't talk to you before then….
以防在那之前沒機會跟你講話……。

A quick reminder before I let you go….
放你走之前很快提醒你一下……。

Don't forget about the dinner next Friday.
別忘了下星期五要一起吃晚餐。

➡ **你也可以這樣說**

Don't forget to e-mail those documents to me.
別忘了將那些文件寄到我的電子信箱。

Don't forget to tell Jason about the meeting on Thursday.
別忘了告訴傑森星期四要開會。

Don't tell anyone else what I told you yet.
我跟你說的事先不要告訴其他人喔。

Ending a call when the callee is busy

對方忙碌時，結束電話

Greg: Things sound pretty hectic over there, Tammy.

Tammy: Yeah. We're working on a big project.

Greg: OK. I won't keep you, then.

Tammy: All right, Greg. I'll talk to you later.

貴格：妳那邊聽起來滿熱鬧的喔，譚美。

譚美：對啊。我們在進行一個大案子。

貴格：好吧，那我就不吵妳了。

譚美：好的，貴格。以後再聊囉。

Things sound pretty hectic over there.
妳那邊聽起來滿熱鬧的喔。

➡ **你也可以這樣說**

It sounds pretty busy over there.
你那邊聽起來滿忙的。

It sounds like things are busy at your office.
你的辦公室那邊聽起來很忙的樣子。

It sounds like you have a lot on your plate.
你聽起來手上事情很多的樣子。

 **I won't keep you, then.**
那我就不吵妳了。

➡ **你也可以這樣說**

I won't take up any more of your time.
我就不繼續佔用你的時間了。

I'll let you go, then.
那我就放你走吧。

I'll let you get back to work, then.
那我就讓你回去工作吧。

Listening

聽力練習 MP3 084

請聽 3 通電話,判斷電話中的兩人將在哪一天碰面,將地點代碼填入正確的日期。

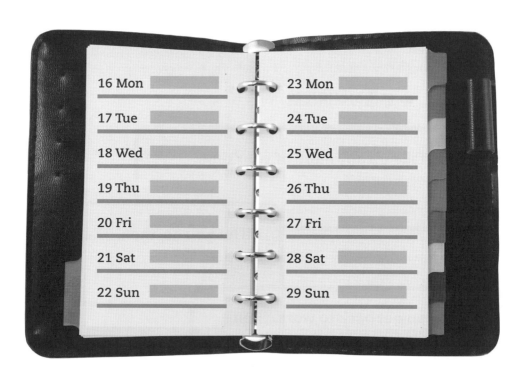

16 Mon		23 Mon	
17 Tue		24 Tue	
18 Wed		25 Wed	
19 Thu		26 Thu	
20 Fri		27 Fri	
21 Sat		28 Sat	
22 Sun		29 Sun	

Answers & Scripts
聽力練習解答與翻譯

▶ 答案

❶

(17 Tue) E

❷

(26 Thu) D

❸

(28 Sat) A

▶ 聽力稿

M: So you'll be arriving in town on Wednesday the 25th, right?
妳二十五日星期三會到這裡，對吧？

W: Actually, my flight's been rescheduled to Thursday morning.
其實，我的班機改到星期四早上了。

M: Oh. Will you be arriving in time to meet for lunch?
喔，那妳趕得上碰面吃午餐嗎？

W: Yeah, it's an early flight. Should we meet in the hotel lobby?
可以，那是早班飛機。我們要在飯店大廳碰面嗎？

M: How about meeting at that place across the street we ate at last time?
要不要約在對街我們上次吃的那家店？

W: Sounds great. Is noon OK?
不錯啊。約中午可以嗎？

M: It's a date!
就這麼說定了！

W: Hi, Andrew. I'm just calling to confirm our meeting on Tuesday the 17th.
嗨，安德魯。我只是打來確認我們十七日星期二的會議。

M: Didn't we change it to Wednesday the 18th?
我們不是改到十八日星期三嗎？

W: We did, but then we changed it back again.
我們是改過，但後來又改回去了。

M: Oh, right. Good thing you called to confirm, Naomi. We're meeting at 2:00, right?
喔，對耶。還好妳有打來確認，娜歐蜜。我們是兩點開會，對吧？

W: Right. Should I just take the elevator up?
是的。我直接搭電梯上去嗎？

M: Yeah. We're on the 5th floor to the right. Just tell the receptionist you're here to see me.
對。我們在五樓的右邊。直接跟接待人員說妳要找我就行了。

W: When is your train arriving, Josh?
賈許，你的火車幾點到啊？

M: At 11:58 in the evening on the 27th.
二十七日晚上十一點五十八分。

W: Wow, that's late. Do you want me to pick you up at the station?
哇，那麼晚。要我開車去火車站接你嗎？

M: Well, I can take the subway downtown.
嗯，我可以搭地鐵到市中心。

W: OK, I'll pick you up there, then.
好，那我就到那邊載你。

M: Thanks, Suzanne. I really appreciate it.
多謝了，蘇珊。非常感激。

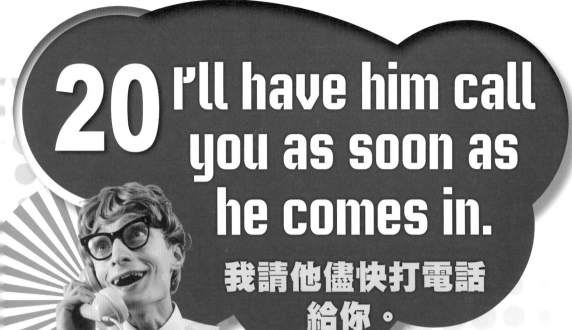

20 I'll have him call you as soon as he comes in.

我請他儘快打電話給你。

翻開下一頁之前，請先播放 **MP3 085**

➡ 閉上眼睛聆聽內容

➡ 再次播放，開始進行逐句跟讀

➡ 專心模仿語調強弱和韻律，要與示範完全相符

➡ 多練習幾遍，直到能以相同速度一字不漏說出每個句子

完成逐句跟讀！請翻開下一頁，進行今天的課程

➡ **Situation 1** 轉告他人回電

➡ **Situation 2** 告知對方聯絡方式

➡ 聽力練習

Situation 1

Getting back to a caller

MP3
086

轉告他人回電

Linda: Hi. My name is Linda Beck, and I'm calling to see if my loan has been approved.

John: Can you hold a moment, please?

Linda: Sure.

John: *[later]* Hi, Linda. Your loan officer is out at the moment. I'll have him call you as soon as he comes in.

Linda: OK. Thank you.

琳達：嗨。我是琳達貝克，我打電話來看看我的貸款核准了沒。

約翰：請在線上稍候，好嗎？

琳達：好的。

約翰：（稍後）嗨，琳達。妳的貸款專員目前外出。我請他進公司儘快打電話給妳。

琳達：好的。謝謝。

Your loan officer is out at the moment. I'll have him call you as soon as he comes in.
妳的貸款專員目前外出。我請他進公司儘快打電話給妳。

➡ **你也可以這樣說**

The person in charge isn't in. Shall I have him call you back?
負責人不在。要我請他回電給你嗎？

Your application is still being processed. We'll call you as soon as a decision is made.
你的申請還在處理中。一有結果我們會馬上打電話給你。

I don't have that information at hand. Can I get back to you a little later?
我手邊沒有資料，可以晚一點再回電給你嗎？

Situation 2

Telling someone how to contact you MP3 087

告知對方聯絡方式

David: Could you let me know when you get the item in stock?

Mary: Of course. How would you like us to get in touch with you?

David: Could you call me at my office? The number is 543-2281, extension 241.

大衛：那個產品有貨的時候可以通知我嗎？

瑪麗：當然。你要我怎麼跟你聯絡？

大衛：可以打到我的辦公室嗎？電話號碼是 543-2281，分機 241。

Could you call me at my office? The number is 543-2281, extension 241.
可以打到我的辦公室嗎？電話號碼是 543-2281，分機 241。

➡ **你也可以這樣說**

Could you call me on my cell phone? My number is 860-475-2690.
你可以打我的手機嗎？電話號碼是 860-475-2690。

Could you leave a message on my answering machine? The number is 685-4496.

可以在我的答錄機留言嗎？電話號碼是 **685-4496**。

Could you fax me? The number is 295-4791.

可以傳真給我嗎？傳真機號碼是 **295-4791**。

Could you e-mail me? My e-mail address is dbarry@mailserve.com.

可以用電子郵件寄給我嗎？我的電子信箱是 dbarry@mailserve.com。

Listening
聽力練習  MP3 088

請聽完 3 通電話，並根據通話內容，在答案框中填入正確答案。

❶

❷

Login ✕

Username:

Password:

☐ Remember Me
☐ Forgot Your Password? Click here.

Submit

Register

❸

Answers & Scripts

聽力練習解答與翻譯

答案

➊

510-268-2824

聽力稿

M: Hi, Susan. This is Thomas.
嗨，蘇珊。我是湯馬斯。

W: Hi, Thomas. Do you have that price list ready for me?
嗨，湯馬斯。你要給我的價目表好了嗎？

M: Yeah. That's why I'm calling. How would you like me to send it to you?
好了。所以我才打電話來。我要怎麼寄給妳？

W: Why don't you fax it to me? The number is 510-268-2824.
傳真給我不就好了？號碼是 510-268-2824。

M: OK. I'll fax it over right away.
好，我馬上傳真過去。

➋

steev
steve6872

W: Hi, Steven. Do you have a copy of the marketing report? The boss wants to see it.
嗨，史蒂芬。你有行銷報告的副本嗎？老闆想要看。

M: Yeah. I have a copy on my computer. Let me give you my username and password.
有。我電腦裡有一份。我給妳使用者名稱和密碼。

W: Just a sec. Let me grab a pen and paper…OK, go ahead.
等一下喔，我拿枝筆和紙……。好了，說吧。

M: My username is S-T-E-E-V, and my password is S-T-E-V-E-6-8-7-2.
我的使用者名稱是 S-T-E-E-V，我的密碼是 S-T-E-V-E-6-8-7-2。

W: Got it. Thanks, Steven.
我知道了。多謝了，史蒂芬。

➌

jabarrett@inksys.com

M: Hello?
喂？

W: Hi, Charles. This is Karen.
嗨，查爾斯。我是凱倫。

M: Hey, Karen. What's up?
嘿，凱倫。怎麼樣啊？

W: I was wondering if you had any contact information for Jack Barrett. I want to invite him to the conference next month.
我想知道你有沒有傑克巴瑞特的聯絡方式。我想要邀請他參加下個月的會議。

M: Let's see…I have his e-mail address. Will that do?
我看看喔……我有他的電子信箱。這個可以嗎？

W: Yeah. That's fine.
可以。沒問題。

M: OK. It's J-A-B-A-R-R-E-T-T at I-N-K-S-Y-S dot com.
好。是 jabarrett@inksys.com。

W: Great. Thanks a lot, Charles.
太好了。多謝了，查爾斯。

21

I don't think I can make it to work today.

我今天沒辦法進公司上班了。

翻開下一頁之前，請先播放 **MP3 089**

➡ 閉上眼睛聆聽內容

➡ 再次播放，開始進行逐句跟讀

➡ 專心模仿語調強弱和韻律，要與示範完全相符

➡ 多練習幾遍，直到能以相同速度一字不漏說出每個句子

完成逐句跟讀！請翻開下一頁，進行今天的課程

➡ **Situation 1** 打電話請假

➡ **Situation 2** 打電話報告行蹤

➡ 聽力練習

Situation 1
Calling in sick/Asking for time off
打電話請假

Tony: Hi, Brenda. This is Tony.

Brenda: Hi, Tony. What's wrong?

Tony: I've come down with the flu.

Brenda: Oh, no.

Tony: Yeah. I don't think I can make it to work today.

湯　尼：嗨，布蘭達。我是湯尼。

布蘭達：嗨，湯尼。怎麼了嗎？

湯　尼：我感冒了。

布蘭達：糟糕。

湯　尼：是啊。我今天沒辦法進公司上班了。

I've come down with the flu.
我感冒了。

➡ 你也可以這樣說

I have a bad cold.
我嚴重感冒。

I'm running a fever.
我發燒了。

I'm feeling under the weather.
我身體不舒服。

My car got towed.
我的車被拖走了。

I got in a fender bender.
我出了個小車禍。

I missed my train.
我沒趕上火車。

 **I don't think I can make it to work today.**
我今天沒辦法進公司上班了。

➡️ **你也可以這樣說**

I won't be able to make it in today.
我今天沒辦法進公司了。

I need to take the day off.
我今天得請假。

I'd like to take the morning off.
我上午要請假。

I'll try to make it in later.
我晚點會儘量趕到。

Calling to say where you are

MP3 091

打電話報告行蹤

Julie: Hi, Nathan. This is Julie.

Nathan: Hi, Julie.

Julie: Listen. I'm just calling to say that I'm stuck in traffic.

Nathan: Oh, OK. Thanks for letting us know.

Julie: Sure. I should be back at the office in half an hour.

茱莉：嗨，納森。我是茱莉。

納森：嗨，茱莉。

茱莉：我跟妳說，我只是打來說一聲我塞在路上。

納森：喔，好的。謝謝妳通知我們。

茱莉：應該的。我應該再過半小時會回到公司。

I'm just calling to say that I'm stuck in traffic.
我只是打來說一聲我塞在路上。

➡ **你也可以這樣說**

I'm calling to say that my meeting is running late.
我打來說一聲，我的會議拖到有點晚。

I just wanted to let you know that I'm meeting with a client.

我是要通知你，我正在與一個客戶碰面。

I just wanted to tell you that I'm out on a business call.

我只是想跟你說一聲，我出來拜訪一個客戶。

I'm just calling to say that I'm out running an errand.

我只是打電話來說一聲，我出來辦點事。

I'm just calling to tell you that I'm at the post office.

我打來跟你說一聲，我在郵局。

Listening
聽力練習 MP3 092

請聽對話判斷 A、B、C 三樣文件收在哪裡（1 ～ 6）。

Ⓐ letter

Ⓑ invoice

Ⓒ sales report

Answers & Scripts
聽力練習解答與翻譯

▶ 答案

Ⓐ letter ❹
Ⓑ invoice ❸
Ⓒ sales report ❺

▶ 聽力稿

W: Hi, Jeff. This is Evelyn.
嗨，杰夫。我是依芙琳。

M: Hi, Evelyn. You don't sound so good.
嗨，依芙琳。妳聽起來身體不太舒服。

W: Yeah. I'm running a high fever. I don't think I can make it in today.
是啊。我發高燒。我今天沒辦法進公司了。

M: I'm sorry to hear that. Is there anything I can do for you?
真替妳感到難過。有什麼我幫得上忙的嗎？

W: Actually, yes. I have a sales report I'm supposed to give to Mr. Landon today. Could you do that for me?
其實，有的。我有一份業績報告今天應該要給藍登先生。你可以幫我交報告嗎？

M: Sure. Where is it?
好啊。放在哪裡？

W: It's in the file cabinet to the right of my desk, in the second drawer from the top.
在我辦公桌右邊的檔案櫃裡，從上面數來第二個抽屜。

M: OK. Anything else?
好。還有別的嗎？

W: Let's see...yes. There's an invoice I need to give to Michael and a letter I need to mail.
我想想看……有。有一份發票要給麥可，還需要寄一封信。

M: OK. Where are they?
好。放在哪裡？

W: The letter's in the document tray on my desk, and the invoice is in the box on the floor to the left of my desk, in a folder marked Best Industries.
信在我辦公桌上的文件匣裡，發票在我辦公桌左邊地上的箱子裡，一個「貝斯特實業公司」的檔案夾裡面。

22 Could you please connect me to Room 214?

請幫我轉二一四號房好嗎？

翻開下一頁之前，請先播放 MP3 **093**

➡ 閉上眼睛聆聽內容

➡ 再次播放，開始進行逐句跟讀

➡ 專心模仿語調強弱和韻律，要與示範完全相符

➡ 多練習幾遍，直到能以相同速度一字不漏說出每個句子

完成逐句跟讀！請翻開下一頁，進行今天的課程

➡ **Situation 1** 打電話到飯店找人

➡ **Situation 2** 打電話到別家公司找同事

➡ 聽力練習

Situation 1

Calling someone at a hotel

MP3 094

打電話到飯店找人

Receptionist: Grand Hotel. How may I help you?

Bert: Hi. **Can you please connect me with Marco Bowen in Room 214?**

Receptionist: Certainly, sir. One moment, please.

總機：華麗飯店。有什麼可以效勞的？

伯特：嗨。請幫我轉二一四號房的馬可波溫好嗎？

總機：好的，先生。請稍候。

Can you please connect me with Marco Bowen in Room 214?
請幫我轉二一四號房的馬可波溫好嗎？

➡️ **你也可以這樣說**

Could you please connect me to Room 214?
請幫我轉二一四號房好嗎？

Can you transfer me to Room 214, please?
請幫我轉二一四號房好嗎？

I'd like to speak to Marco Bowen in Room 214, please.

我想要找二一四號房的馬可波溫。

I'd like to send a fax to Marco Bowen in Room 214. Could you please tell me the fax number?

我要傳真給二一四號房的馬可波溫。請告訴我傳真機號碼好嗎？

Calling a colleague at another company

打電話到別家公司找同事

Receptionist: Sales Department. How can I help you?

Janis: Hi. This is Janis French at Edison Scientific.
I'm calling for my colleague Gerald Sparks,
who's attending a meeting in your department.

Receptionist: OK, Ms. French. Please hold while I put you through.

總　　機：業務部。有什麼可以效勞的？

珍妮絲：嗨。我是愛迪生科技公司的珍妮絲法蘭屈。我打電話來找同事傑洛史巴克，他到貴部門參加一個會議。

總　　機：好的，法藍屈小姐。請在線上稍候，我幫妳轉接。

I'm calling for my colleague Gerald Sparks, who's attending a meeting in your department.
我打電話來找同事傑洛史巴克，他到貴部門參加一個會議。

➡ 你也可以這樣說

Could you connect me with Gerald Sparks, please? I'm a coworker of his.
請幫我轉接傑洛史巴克好嗎？我是他的同事。

**Can I please speak to Gerald Sparks?
He's at your office on business.**

我可以找傑洛史巴克嗎？他在貴公司洽公。

**I'm looking for my colleague Gerald Sparks.
He said he would be at your office today.**

我要找我的同事傑洛史巴克。他說他今天會在貴公司。

❶ [   ] What time is it now?

聽力練習 MP3 096

聽 3 通電話，根據通話內容回答問題。

❶ [   ] What is the extension number for Kara Flynn's room?
卡拉佛林的房間分機號碼是幾號？

Ⓐ 0216 ○二一六
Ⓑ 0215 ○二一五
Ⓒ 216 二一六
Ⓓ 215 二一五

❷ [   ] What will the man likely do next?
那位男士接下來會怎麼做？

Ⓐ Connect the woman with Mr. Hardin 將女士的電話轉接給哈丁先生
Ⓑ Tell the woman Mr. Hardin's room number 告訴女士哈丁先生的房號
Ⓒ Take the woman's phone number 記下女士的電話號碼
Ⓓ Ask the woman for her room number 詢問女士的房號

❸ [   ] When will the man probably call Mr. Baxter?
那位男士可能會在幾點打給巴斯特先生？

Ⓐ At 8:00 4a.m. 早上八點
Ⓑ At 10:00 p.m. 晚上十點
Ⓒ At 10:30 p.m. 晚上十點半
Ⓓ Late at night 深夜

Answers & Scripts
聽力練習解答與翻譯

答案

1   B

2   C

3   A

聽力稿

M: Hi. Could you please connect me with Kara Flynn in Room 215?
請幫我轉二一五號房的卡拉佛林好嗎？

W: Sure, one moment. *[pause]* I'm sorry, there's no answer.
好的，請稍候。（過了一下）抱歉，沒人接聽。

M: OK, thank you. I'll try again later.
好吧，謝謝。我晚點再打來看看。

W: Oh, by the way—you can call her room directly if you like. The extension number is just the room number with a zero in front of it.
喔，順帶一提——如果你要的話，可以直接撥到她的房間。分機號碼就是在房號前面加一個零。

M: Oh, that's good to know. Thanks a lot!
喔，很有用的資訊。多謝了！

W: Hello. I'd like to speak to Glen Hardin. He's a guest at your hotel.
喂，我要找葛蘭哈丁。他是投宿貴飯店的房客。

M: Do you know his room number, ma'am?
小姐，妳知道他的房號嗎？

W: I'm afraid not. He's a client of mine, and he's in town on business. Could you tell me what room he's in?
恐怕不知道。他是我的客戶，是來出差的。你能告訴我他住哪一間房嗎？

M: I'm afraid that's against hotel policy. If you leave your number I can make sure he gets it, though.
那會違反公司的規定。但是如果妳留下妳的電話號碼，我一定會轉交給他。

W: OK. That would be great.
好啊。那就太好了。

M: Hi. Could you transfer me to Scott Baxter in Room 522, please?
嗨，請幫我轉五二二號房的史考特巴斯特好嗎？

W: Of course. Just a moment. *[pause]* Sorry, sir. He appears to be out.
好的。請稍候。（過了一下）抱歉，先生。他似乎外出了。

M: Hmm, let's see—it's 9:30 now. He usually doesn't stay out too late, so I'll try again in an hour.
嗯，我想想看——現在九點半。他通常不會在外面待到太晚，我一個小時之後再打來看看。

W: Actually, our switchboard closes at 10:00, and won't open again until 8:00 a.m.
其實，我們的轉接櫃臺十點關閉，明天早上八點才會再開。

M: Oh, I see. I'll give him a wake-up call then.
喔，我懂了。那我明天一早打來叫他起床吧。

23 Please leave a message after the tone...

聽到訊號聲請留言⋯⋯

翻開下一頁之前，請先播放 MP3 **097**

➡ 閉上眼睛聆聽內容

➡ 再次播放，開始進行逐句跟讀

➡ 專心模仿語調強弱和韻律，要與示範完全相符

➡ 多練習幾遍，直到能以相同速度一字不漏說出每個句子

完成逐句跟讀！請翻開下一頁，進行今天的課程

➡ **Situation 1/2** 請來電者在答錄機留言、在他人答錄機留言

➡ **Situation 3/4** 答錄機招呼語、總機招呼語

➡ 聽力練習

Asking someone to leave a message

請來電者在答錄機留言

Frank: Hello. You've reached the voice mail of Frank Hardy. I'm sorry I missed your call. **Please leave your name, number and a brief message, and I'll get back to you as soon as possible.**

[beep]

Liz: Hi, Frank. This is Liz Johnson at Cambridge Systems. My office number is 427-8356. I'd like to go over the contract terms with you, so please call me back by tomorrow afternoon.

法蘭克：喂。這是法蘭克哈迪的語音信箱。抱歉無法接聽你的電話。請留下姓名、電話號碼及簡短留言，我會盡快回電。

（嗶聲）

麗　茲：嗨，法蘭克。我是劍橋系統公司的麗茲強生。我的辦公室電話是 427-8356。我想跟你一起檢視合約條文，請於明天下午之前回電給我。

Situation 2

Leaving a message

在他人答錄機留言

Don: Please leave a message after the tone.

[beep]

Allan: Hi, Don. This is Allan Waterford. I'm just calling to remind you about our meeting tomorrow morning at ten.

唐　：請在訊號聲之後留言。

（嗶聲）

艾倫：嗨，唐。我是艾倫華德福。我是打來提醒你明天早上十點我們要開會。

Please leave a message after the tone

答錄機招呼語

- **個人手機**

Hi. You've reached Jane Alston at 536-1212. Please leave a message after the tone.

嗨，這裡是珍艾斯頓的電話 536-1212。請在訊號聲之後留言。

- **辦公室分機**

Hello. This is Justin Greenberg in Accounting. I'm away from my desk at the moment. Please leave a message and I'll call you as soon as possible.

喂。我是會計部的賈斯汀葛林伯格。我目前離開座位。請留下訊息，我會盡快回電。

- **住家**

Hi. You've reached the Baker residence. We can't come to the phone right now, so please leave a message after the beep.

嗨。這裡是貝克家。我們目前無法接聽電話，請在嗶嗶聲之後留言。

- **因出差、度假會較長時間不在**

Hi. You've reached the office of Barry Mullins. I'm away on vacation until August 24th. Please leave your name and number and I'll get back to you when I return.

嗨。這裡是貝瑞穆林的辦公室。我去度假到八月二十四日回來。請留下姓名電話，我回來之後會回電。

Situation 4
Please leave a message after the tone

總機招呼語

- ### 現在是下班時間……

  Thank you for calling Reliable Life Insurance. We are currently unavailable to take your call. Our business hours are nine a.m. to six p.m., Monday through Friday. If you'd like to leave a message, please press the extension of the person you're trying to reach. Or you can press zero to leave a message for our receptionist.

  感謝您致電瑞來保人壽。我們現在無法接聽您的電話。我們的上班時間是週一到週五，上午九點到下午六點。如果您要留言，請直撥分機號碼或撥○留言給總機。

Listening
聽力練習 MP3 102

請聽光碟中的答錄機內容，回答以下 **3** 個問題。

❶ ⬜⬜⬜ What type of business is this recording for?
這段語音是出自於哪一種公司？

Ⓐ A phone company 電話公司

Ⓑ A bank 銀行

Ⓒ A call center 電話行銷公司

Ⓓ An accounting firm 會計事務所

❷ ⬜⬜⬜ What should a caller who wishes to visit the business do?
想前往該公司洽公的人應該怎麼做？

Ⓐ Press 1 按一

Ⓑ Press 2 按二

Ⓒ Press 3 按三

Ⓓ Press 4 按四

❸ ⬜⬜⬜ What should a caller do to speak to an actual person?
想跟人直接通話的來電者應該怎麼做？

Ⓐ Hang up and dial again 掛斷電話再撥一次

Ⓑ Dial customer service 打客服專線

Ⓒ Call during business hours 上班時間再來電

Ⓓ Remain on the line 在線上等候

聽力練習解答與翻譯

▶ 答案

①

B

②

A

③

D

▶ 聽力稿

Thank you for calling Northwest Savings. To hear about our business hours, please press one. For account information, please press two. To transfer funds or pay bills by phone, please press three. If you wish to speak to one of our customer representatives, please stay on the line, and your call will be answered in the order in which it was received.

感謝您致電西北儲蓄銀行。想知道我們的營業時間，請按一。開戶資訊，請按二。電話轉帳或付款，請按三。如果要與客服人員通話，請在線上稍候，您的電話會依來電順序接通。

電話關鍵句中文索引

 打電話到朋友家 p.10

 打電話到朋友的手機 p.12

打電話到辦公室找人   p.18

- 哈囉。麻煩一下，我可以跟艾倫羅傑斯說話嗎？
  Hello. May I speak to Alan Rogers, please?

- 嗯。我要找艾倫羅傑斯。
  Yes. I'm calling for Alan Rogers.

- 嗯。請幫我轉接艾倫羅傑斯好嗎？
  Yes. Can you connect me with Alan Rogers, please?

- 嗨。可以幫我轉接艾倫羅傑斯嗎？
  Hi. Can you please put me through to Alan Rogers?

- 哈囉。我可以跟會計部的艾倫羅傑斯講話嗎？
  Hello. Can I speak to Alan Rogers in Accounting?

- 嗯。可以幫我轉分機一三七嗎？
  Yes. Can you please connect me to extension 137?

- 嗨。我是先進軟體公司的鮑伯戴維斯。艾倫羅傑斯在嗎？
  Hi. This is Bob Davis at Advanced Software. Is Alan Rogers in?

請對方轉接客服   p.20

- 嗯。我要跟客服人員講話。
  Yes. I need to talk to a customer service rep.

- 嗯。我有一個客服相關的問題。
  Yes. I have a customer service question.

- 嗨。可以幫我轉客服部嗎？
  Hi. Can you connect me with customer service?

- 可以幫我轉貴公司的客服部嗎？
  Could you connect me with your customer service department?

- 嗨。我有訂閱相關的問題。可以幫我轉客服部嗎？
  Hi. I have a question about my subscription. Can you put me though to customer service?

要找的人不在，晚點再打　　　　　　　　p.74

- 我明天再打。
- 我打他的手機。
- 你有他的手機號碼嗎？
- 能把他的手機號碼給我嗎？
  這件事很急。
- 我有什麼方法可以跟他聯絡嗎？

- 我什麼時候打電話比較合適？
- 你知道他什麼時候會回來嗎？
- 他預計什麼時候回來？

I'll call again tomorrow.
I'll try his cell phone.
Do you have his cell phone number?
Could you tell me his cell phone number?
It's rather urgent.
Is there some way I could get in touch with
him?
When would be a good time for me to call?
Do you know when he'll be back?
When do you expect him back?

 ## 請對方轉接電話給其他人　　　　　　　　p.76

- 那麼，幫我轉接他的主管好嗎？

- 請幫我轉接業務部其他的人好嗎？

- 有其他人可以幫我嗎？
- 有其他人可以跟我討論（這件事）
  嗎？
- 這樣的話，我該跟誰討論
  （這件事）？

Could you connect me with his supervisor
then?
Could you please transfer me to someone
else in Sales?
Is there someone else who could help me?
Is there someone else I could talk to
(about…)?
In that case, who should I speak to
(about…)?

總機轉接電話 p.90

- 嗨,凱倫。戴爾吉布森在一線找妳。

  Hi, Karen. You have a call from Dale Gibson on line one.

- 羅伯特,線上有一位辛普森小姐找你。

  Robert, there's a Ms. Simpson on the line for you.

- 韋伯先生,波特先生在二線等你。

  Mr. Webb, Mr. Porter is waiting for you on line two.

- 史蒂文貝克公司的馬修史蒂文來電找你。

  You have a call from Matthew Stevens at Stevens & Baker.

- 有一位鮑伯卡特在線上。要我轉接過去嗎?

  There's a Bob Carter on the line. Should I put him through?

 部門間轉接電話 p.92

- 線上有一位叫芭芭拉裴瑞茲的女士找你。

  There's a woman on the line named Barbara Perez for you.

- 我這邊有一位包威爾運動用品的採購在線上,他對我們的新產品有一些問題。

  I have a buyer from Powell Sports on the line with some questions about our new products.

- 我是業務部的亞當寇門。我接到一通包威爾運動用品的電話,要問一個請款單的問題。

  This is Adam Coleman in Sales. I have a call from Powell Sports about an invoice.

- 包威爾運動用品的瓊斯先生來電,他有一個關於請款單的問題。要我把他轉給你嗎?

  Mr. Jones at Powell Sports has a question about an invoice. Should I transfer him to you?

告知有緊急電話

p.99

- 你有一通電話,是內華達金融公司的
  塔克先生打來的。他說是要緊的事。

  You have a call from Mr. Tucker at Nevada Finance. He says it's important.

- 抱歉打擾了。瑞克派瑞在二線,他說
  有急事。

  Sorry to interrupt. Rick Perry is on line two and he says it's an emergency.

- 傑克蕭說他必須馬上跟你談一談。要
  我把電話轉給你嗎?

  Jack Shaw says he needs to talk to you right away. Should I put him through?

- 我知道你說過要幫你擋電話,但執行
  長在線上要找你。

  I know you told me to hold your calls, but the CEO is on the line for you.

 ## 告知有私人電話

p.100

- 你太太打電話來,詹姆士。

  You have a call from your wife, James.

- 詹姆士,你弟弟在線上。

  James, your brother is on the phone.

- 你的女兒從倫敦打電話來,詹姆士。

  Your daughter is calling from London, James.

- 一線有你的私人電話。

  You have a personal call on line one.

- 要我跟對方說你在開會嗎?

  Should I say you're in a meeting?

- 要我跟她說你不在位子上嗎?

  Shall I tell her you're away from your desk?

- 我跟她說你很忙,但她說有急事。

  I said you were busy, but she says it's urgent.

- 如果你要的話,我可以跟她說你
  外出了。

  I can tell her you're out if you like.

請對方回電 p.106

- 他回來時請他打電話給我。 Please tell him to call me when he returns.
- 請他回來時打電話到我的公司給我好嗎？ Could you have him call me at my office when he gets back?
- 請他打電話到我的公司好嗎？我會待到六點半。 Can you have him call me at my office? I'll be here till 6:30.
- 請他打我的手機好嗎？ Could you please tell him to call me on my cell phone?
- 請他儘快打電話給我。 Tell him to please call me as soon as possible.
- 請轉告他今天下午打 867-5309 這支電話給我。 Please tell him to call me at 867-5309 this afternoon.

 ## 請人轉告消息 p.108

- 請轉告她訂的東西可以取貨了。 Please tell her that her order is ready to pick up.
- 請轉告她，我傳真了一份文件給她，想確認她有收到。 Tell her I sent her a fax and just wanted to confirm that she'd received it.
- 我寄了一份報告給她，請她查一下電子郵件信箱。 I sent her a report by e-mail, so please tell her to check her inbox.
- 請轉告她，我收到她的傳真／電子郵件了，好嗎？ Could you let her know that I received her fax/e-mail?
- 請轉告她明天的會議取消了。 Please tell her that tomorrow's meeting has been canceled.
- 可以轉告她會議從兩點半改到三點半嗎？ Could you tell her that the meeting's been moved from 2:30 to 3:30?
- 請跟她說會議地點改了。我稍晚會用電子郵件寄地圖給她。 Please tell her that the location of the meeting has changed. I'll e-mail her a map later.

撥打緊急電話 p.114

- 我必須馬上跟他談。
  I need to talk to him right away.
- 我必須立刻與他取得聯繫。
  I need to get in touch with him immediately.
- 這件事很緊急。
  This really can't wait.
- 你知道我該怎麼跟他聯絡嗎?
  Do you know how I can contact him?
- 我可以打其他電話找到他嗎?
  Is there another number I can reach him at?
- 可以給我他的手機號碼嗎?
  Could you give me his cell phone number?

首次致電給某人 p.116

- 我是強生辦公用品的業務代表,我想通知他一個特別優惠。
  I'm a sales rep at Johnson Supplies, and I'd like to tell him about a special offer.
- 他在一個商展上給我名片,要我打電話給他。
  He gave me his card at a trade show and asked me to call.
- 我是一支運動隊伍的代表,我想跟他談一個贊助案。
  I represent a sports team, and I'd like to discuss a sponsorship deal with him.
- 我服務於「不再飢餓」組織,想知道他是否願意捐款。
  I work for No More Hunger, and I'm wondering if he'd like to make a donation.
- 這裡是大都會人壽,我想跟他談一下他的保險涵蓋範圍。
  I'm with Metropolitan Life, and I'd like to discuss his insurance coverage.

表明來電用意是回電　　　　　　　　　　p.122

- 柯爾小姐請我回電給她。
  Ms. Kerr asked me to return her call.
- 柯爾小姐留言要我回電。
  Ms. Kerr left me a message asking me to call her back.
- 她留言要我兩點之後回電。
  She left a message asking me to call her after 2:00.
- 我沒接到她打到我手機的電話，所以我回撥給她。
  I missed her call on my cell phone, so I'm calling her back.
- 她在我外出時來電，我回她電話。
  She called me when I was out, so I'm returning her call.

 再次致電　　　　　　　　　　　　　　p.124

- 我稍早來電過，但電話忙線中。
  I called earlier, but the line was busy.
- 我今天早上有來電，他請我兩點再打來。
  I called this morning, and he asked me to call back at 2:00.
- 賀門先生用完午餐回來了嗎？
  Is Mr. Herman back from lunch yet?
- 賀門先生回到座位了嗎？
  Is Mr. Herman back at his desk yet?

 再次確認聯絡方式 p.131

- 我打過電話給他，但那個電話是空號。
  I tried calling him, but the number is no longer in service.
- 我打過電話給他，但那已經不是他的號碼。
  I tried calling, but he's no longer at that number.
- 我打過電話給他，但一直電話中。
  I tried calling him, but I kept getting a busy signal.
- 那個電話一直電話中。妳有他的其他電話嗎？
  The line is always busy. Do you have another number for him?
- 我應該是抄錯電話號碼了。妳可以再給我一次嗎？
  I think I wrote the number wrong. Could you give it to me again?

 打電話先寒暄幾句 p.132

- 你好嗎？
  How are you?
- 你都還順利吧？
  How are things with you?
- 你的生意如何？
  How's business?
- 一切都還好吧？
  How's everything?
- 現在打給你合適嗎？
  Is this a good time for you?
- 希望我沒有打擾到你。
  I hope I'm not disturbing you.
- 你現在有空嗎？
  Do you have a minute?
- 你現在方便說話嗎？
  Can you talk right now?

打電話向對方道謝 p.139

- 上次那個案子謝謝你幫了我。 Thanks for helping me out on that project.
- 真是多謝你上次的大力幫忙。 Thanks for all your help last time.
- 很感謝你幫我那麼多忙。 I really appreciate all the help you've given me.
- 我上次去拜訪時，多謝你的招待。 Thank you for your hospitality when I visited.

 打電話向對方道歉 p.141

- 抱歉拖了這麼久才回電。 I'm sorry for taking so long to return your call.
- 抱歉這麼晚才回覆。 Sorry for getting back to you so late.
- 上次搞錯了真是抱歉。 I'd like to apologize for the mix-up last time.
- 對於上次造成誤會，我要再說一次抱歉。 Sorry again for that misunderstanding.

打 電話
關鍵句

 結束電話前的提醒 p.154

- 趁你還在線上……。 While I still have you on the line….
- 以防在那之前沒機會跟你講話……。 In case I don't talk to you before then….
- 放你走之前很快提醒你一下……。 A quick reminder before I let you go….
- 別忘了將那些文件寄到我的電子信箱。 Don't forget to e-mail those documents to me.
- 別忘了告訴傑森星期四要開會。 Don't forget to tell Jason about the meeting on Thursday.
- 我跟你說的事先不要告訴其他人喔。 Don't tell anyone else what I told you yet.

 對方忙碌時，結束電話 p.156

- 你那邊聽起來滿忙的。 It sounds pretty busy over there.
- 你的辦公室那邊聽起來很忙的樣子。 It sounds like things are busy at your office.
- 你聽起來手上事情很多的樣子。 It sounds like you have a lot on your plate.
- 我就不繼續佔用你的時間了。 I won't take up any more of your time.
- 那我就放你走吧。 I'll let you go, then.
- 那我就讓你回去工作吧。 I'll let you get back to work, then.

電話美語 Hold 的住 < 203

打電話請假 p.170

- 我嚴重感冒。
- 我發燒了。
- 我身體不舒服。
- 我的車被拖走了。
- 我出了個小車禍。
- 我沒趕上火車。
- 我今天沒辦法進公司了。
- 我今天得請假。
- 我上午要請假。
- 我晚點會儘量趕到。

I have a bad cold.
I'm running a fever.
I'm feeling under the weather.
My car got towed.
I got in a fender bender.
I missed my train.
I won't be able to make it in today.
I need to take the day off.
I'd like to take the morning off.
I'll try to make it in later.

 ## 打電話報告行蹤 p.172

- 我打來說一聲，我的會議拖到有點晚。
- 我是要通知你，我正在與一個客戶碰面。
- 我只是想跟你說一聲，我出來拜訪一個客戶。
- 我只是打電話來說一聲，我出來辦點事。
- 我打來跟你說一聲，我在郵局。

I'm calling to say that my meeting is running late.
I just wanted to let you know that I'm meeting with a client.
I just wanted to tell you that I'm out on a business call.
I'm just calling to say that I'm out running an errand.
I'm just calling to tell you that I'm at the post office.

 ## 打電話到飯店找人 p.178

- 請幫我轉二一四號房好嗎？
- 請幫我轉二一四號房好嗎？
- 我想要找二一四號房的馬可波溫。

- 我要傳真給二一四號房的馬可波溫。
  請告訴我傳真機號碼好嗎？

Could you please connect me to Room 214?

Can you transfer me to Room 214, please?

I'd like to speak to Marco Bowen in Room 214, please.

I'd like to send a fax to Marco Bowen in Room 214. Could you please tell me the fax number?

 ## 打電話到別家公司找同事 p.180

- 請幫我轉接傑洛史巴克好嗎？我是他的同事。
- 我可以找傑洛史巴克嗎？他在貴公司洽公。
- 我要找我的同事傑洛史巴克。他說他今天會在貴公司。

Could you connect me with Gerald Sparks, please? I'm a coworker of his.

Can I please speak to Gerald Sparks? He's at your office on business.

I'm looking for my colleague Gerald Sparks. He said he would be at your office today.

告知對方聯絡方式　　　　　　　　　　　　p.164

- 你可以打我的手機嗎？電話號碼是
  860-475-2690。

  Could you call me on my cell phone?
  My number is 860-475-2690.

- 可以在我的答錄機留言嗎？電話號碼
  是 **685-4496**。

  Could you leave a message on my answering
  machine? The number is 685-4496.

- 可以傳真給我嗎？傳真機號碼是
  295-4791。

  Could you fax me? The number is 295-4791.

- 可以用電子郵件寄給我嗎？我的電子
  信箱是 **dbarry@mailserve.com**。

  Could you e-mail me? My e-mail address is
  dbarry@mailserve.com.

接聽打來公司的電話 p.26

- 喂。泰坦保險公司。感謝您耐心等候。
  Hello. This is Titan Insurance. Thank you for waiting.
- 喂。理賠部。
  Hello. Claims Department.
- 泰坦保險公司。我是梅姬。
  Titan Insurance. Maggie speaking.
- 喂。我是梅姬奧柏林。
  Hello. Maggie Oberlin.
- 理賠部。我是梅姬奧柏林。
  Claims Department. This is Maggie Oberlin.
- 感謝您耐心等候。我是梅姬奧柏林。
  Thanks for waiting. I'm Maggie Oberlin.

 ## 詢問有何貴幹 p.28

- 請問有何貴幹？
  How may I help you?
- 請問有何貴幹？
  How can I help you today?
- 請問有何貴幹？
  What can I do for you today?
- 請問你要找誰？
  Who would you like to speak to/with?
- 請問有什麼事？
  What is this in regard to?
- 請問哪裡找？
  Who may I ask is calling?
- 請問貴姓大名？
  May I have your name, please?

告知對方你在忙，稍候回電 p.34

- 抱歉，我正在講一通重要電話。我再打給你好嗎？

  Sorry, I'm taking an important call. Can I call you back?

- 我現在挺忙的。我晚點再打給你好嗎？

  I'm afraid I'm busy right now. Could I call you back later?

- 我正在開會。開完會再打給你好嗎？

  I'm in a meeting now. Can I call when it's over?

- 我正在開車，得晚一點再打給你了。

  I'm driving right now, so I'll have to call you back later.

- 我在搭地鐵／火車。我進公司會打給你。

  I'm on the train now. I'll call you when I get to the office.

- 我大約一個小時後再從公司打給你好嗎？

  Could I call you back from the office in about one hour?

 請對方晚點再打來 p.36

- 你能晚點再打來嗎？

  Could you call back a little later?

- 你能過一個小時再打來嗎？

  Could you call back in an hour?

- 你介意三點左右再打來嗎？

  Would you mind calling back around 3 o'clock?

- 你能明天再打來嗎？

  Could you call again tomorrow?

- 我正要去吃午餐。你能一點之後再打來嗎？

  I was just leaving for lunch. Could you call back after 1:00?

- 你能在四點到五點間再打給我嗎？

  Could you call me back between 4:00 and 5:00?

確認來電者身分 p.42

- 麻煩再說一次您貴姓大名？ / Could you repeat your name, please?
- 您剛剛說您貴姓大名？ / What was your name again, please?
- 抱歉。我沒聽清楚您貴姓大名。 / I'm sorry. I didn't catch your name.
- 請問您是哪家公司，克爾克小姐？ / And what company are you with, Mrs. Kirk?
- 小姐／先生，請問您代表哪家公司？ / What company do you represent, madam/sir?
- 請再說一次您是哪間公司好嗎？ / Could I have the name of your company again?
- 請重複一遍您的大名和公司名稱好嗎？ / Could you please repeat your name and company?

告知來電者你沒聽懂 p.44

- 請講慢一點好嗎？ / Could you speak a little slower, please?
- 抱歉。請你講清楚一點好嗎？ / I'm sorry. Could you speak more clearly, please?
- 請講大聲一點好嗎？ / Could you please speak a little louder?
- 抱歉。我沒聽懂你剛剛說什麼。 / Sorry. I didn't understand what you said.
- 請再說一遍好嗎？ / Could you please repeat that?
- 你那裡有人會說中文／英文嗎？ / Is there someone there who speaks Chinese/English?
- 請在線上稍候，我去找會說英文的人過來。 / Please hold while I get someone who speaks English.
- 我的英文不太好。你能說慢一點嗎？ / My English isn't very good. Could you speak slower?

告知來電者你聽不清楚 p.50

- 我們似乎收訊不良。我再回電話給你好嗎？
  We seem to have a bad connection. Can I call you back?

- 電話雜訊好嚴重。你能重新打電話過來嗎？
  There's a lot of static on the line. Can you call again?

- 電話快要斷訊了。我再打給你吧。
  I think I'm losing you. Let me call you back.

- 抱歉，這裡好吵。我聽不見你說的話。
  Sorry, it's really noisy here. I can't hear what you're saying.

- 這裡太吵了。我聽不見。晚點再打給你好嗎？
  It's too noisy here. I can't hear you. Can I call you later?

- 我聽不見。我用室內電話再撥給你。
  I can't hear you. Let me call you back from a land line.

- 我的電池快沒電了。我換一支電話再撥給你。
  My battery's almost dead. I'll call you back from another phone.

 請對方寄資料給你 p.52

- 請把報告寄一份到電子信箱給我好嗎？
  Could you e-mail me a copy of the report?

- 請寄到電子信箱或傳真一份報價給我好嗎？
  Can you send me a quote by e-mail or fax?

- 我給你我的電子郵件，你能把規格寄給我嗎？
  If I give you my e-mail, could you send me the specs?

- 請把圖表加在電子郵件附件寄給我好嗎？
  Could you please send me the chart in an e-mail attachment?

- 計畫擬妥之後請寄電子郵件給我好嗎？
  Please e-mail the plans to me when they're ready.

幫來電者轉接 p.58

- 請在線上稍候。我幫你轉接。　　　Please hold for a moment. I'll transfer you.
- 請稍候,我幫你轉接。　　　　　　Just a moment, I'll put you through.
- 請稍待一會兒,我幫你轉人力　　　One moment, I'll transfer you to HR.
  資源部。
- 我幫你轉負責人。　　　　　　　　Let me transfer you to the person in charge.
- 我幫你轉業務部的詹姆絲小姐。　　Let me connect you with Ms. James in Sales.
- 好的,我幫你轉業務部。　　　　　All right, let me connect you to Sales.

 告知對方要找的人忙線中 p.60

- 他現在忙線中。　　　　　　　　　His line is busy at the moment.
- 他正在接另一通電話。　　　　　　He's taking another call right now.
- 他正在見一個客戶。　　　　　　　He's with a client at the moment.
- 他正在開會。　　　　　　　　　　He's in a meeting right now.
- 他正在忙。　　　　　　　　　　　He's busy at the moment.
- 他現在不在位子上。　　　　　　　He's not at his desk right now.
- 他現在不能聽電話。　　　　　　　He's not available right now.

請秘書拒接電話 p.66

- 跟他說我出去了好嗎？
  Would you tell him I'm out?

- 跟他說我在開會。
  Just tell him that I'm in a meeting.

- 請跟他說我不在座位上好嗎？
  Could you tell him that I'm away from my desk?

- 請留下他的電話號碼好嗎？我晚點回電給他。
  Could you get his number? I'll call him back later.

- 請跟他說我三十分鐘後回電給他好嗎？
  Would you tell him I'll call him back in 30 minutes?

- 跟他說我一講完電話就打給他。
  Tell him I'll call him as soon as I get off the phone.

 告知對方要找的人不在 p.68

- 她現在不在辦公室。四點之前應該會回來。
  She's not in the office right now. She should be back by 4:00.

- 她外出一下，應該很快就會回來。
  She stepped out for a moment. She should be back soon.

- 她外出吃午餐，一個小時之內會回來。
  She's out to lunch. She'll be back within an hour.

- 她出差去了，要到星期四才會回來。
  She's away on business. She won't be back till Thursday.

- 西爾小姐今天休假。
  I'm afraid Ms. Hill is off today.

- 西爾小姐今天沒來。
  I'm afraid Ms. Hill isn't in today.

- 西爾小姐已經轉調到倫敦辦事處。
  Ms. Hill has been transferred to our London office.

 幫來電者記下留言 p.82

- 需要留言嗎？ — May I take a message?
- 可以請教大名及電話嗎？ — May I have your name and phone number?
- 你要的話，我可以幫你留言。 — I can take a message if you'd like.
- 我重複一次你的留言。 — Let me repeat your message.
- 我唸一遍給你聽。 — Let me read that back to you.
- 好的，湯姆亞當斯，電話 368-8525，對嗎？ — OK, that's Tom Adams at 368-8525, right?
- 湯姆亞當斯，電話 368-8525。正確嗎？ — Tom Adams at 368-8525. Is that correct?
- 電話 368-8525，對嗎？ — 368-8525, right?
- 抱歉。你能再說一次電話號碼嗎？ — I'm sorry. Could you repeat that number?

 確認人名、公司名拼法 p.85

- 請告訴我你的公司名稱怎麼拼好嗎？ — Could you spell your company's name for me?
- 請（再）拼給我聽好嗎？ — Could you please spell that for me (again)?
- 你的姓要怎麼拼？ — How do you spell your last name?
- 你的姓要怎麼拼？ — How is your last name spelled?
- 拼法是 M-E-Y-E-R-S，對嗎？ — That's M-E-Y-E-R-S, right?
- 是 C 開頭的凱西嗎？ — Is that Cathy with a "C"?
- 是貓那個字裡面的「C」嗎？ — Is that "C" as in cat?

指示接待人員如何處理訪客　　　　　　　p.147

- 請告訴他我過一下就去找他。　　Please tell him I'll be with him shortly.
- 請他坐一下，好嗎？　　　　　　Could you ask him to have a seat?
- 請帶他去會議室，好嗎？　　　　Could you please take him to the conference room?
- 請他在會議室等一下，好嗎？　　Could you have him wait in the conference room?
- 請找湯姆艾斯特拉達出去接待他，好嗎？　　Could you ask Tom Estrada to go out and greet him?

要去忙別的事，結束電話　　　　　　　　p.148

- 我現在有點忙。　　　　　　　　I'm a little busy at the moment.
- 我已經要離開了。　　　　　　　I was just leaving.
- 我和客戶在談事情。　　　　　　I'm with a client.
- 這件事我恐怕幫不上忙。　　　　I'm afraid I can't help you with that.
- 你可以晚點再打來嗎？　　　　　Could you call back later?
- 我得晚點再打給你講這件事了。　I'll have to get back to you on that.
- 我幫你把電話轉給另一個人。　　Let me connect you with someone else.
- 如果你留下電話號碼，我可以請人回電給你。　　If you leave your number, I can have someone get back to you.

 轉告他人回電 p.163

- 負責人不在。要我請他回電給你嗎？

  The person in charge isn't in. Shall I have him call you back?

- 你的申請還在處理中。一有結果我們會馬上打電話給你。

  Your application is still being processed. We'll call you as soon as a decision is made.

- 我手邊沒有資料，可以晚一點再回電給你嗎？

  I don't have that information at hand. Can I get back to you a little later?

讀者基本資料

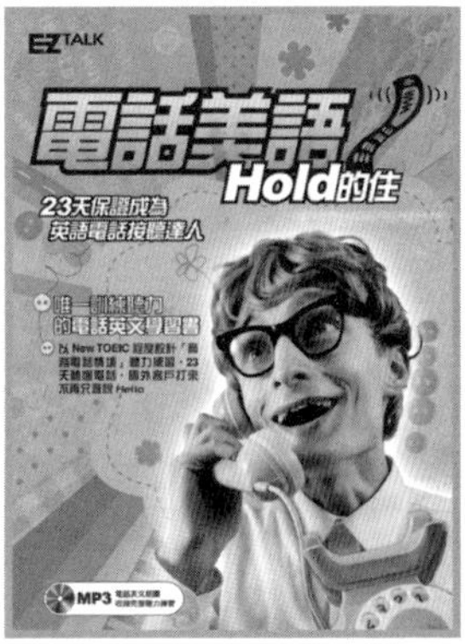

■是否為 EZ TALK 訂戶？　　□是　□否

■姓名 ______________________________ 性別 □男　□女

■生日　民國 __________ 年 __________ 月 __________ 日

■地址　□□□ - □□（請務必填寫郵遞區號）

____

■聯絡電話（日）______________________________

（夜）______________________________

（手機）______________________________

■ E-mail ______________________________

（請務必填寫 E-mail，讓我們為您提供 VIP 服務）

■職業

□學生　□服務業　□傳媒業　□資訊業　□自由業　□軍公教　□出版業

□補教業　□其他

■教育程度

□國中以下　□高中　□專科　□大學　□研究所以上

■您從何種通路購得本書？

□一般書店　□量販店　□網路書店　□書展　□郵局劃撥

您對本書的建議……

請傳真至 *02-2708-5182*，欲索取雜誌（見背面），請裝入信封投郵筒寄回，感謝你的配合！

國家圖書館出版品預行編目資料

電話美語 Hold 的住 / Judd Piggott, Vera Chen 作 .
-- 初版 . -- 臺北市：日月文化，2011.11
224 面，17×23 公分（EZ 叢書館）
ISBN：978-986-248-214-8（平裝）
1. 英文　2. 會話
805.188　　　　　　　　　　　　100019244

EZ 叢書館

電話美語 Hold 的住

作　　者：Judd Piggott, Vera Chen
執行顧問：陳思容
副 總 編：葉瑋玲
總 編 審：Judd Piggott
執行編輯：方文凌，賴建豪
文字編輯：陳彥廷
美術設計：管仕豪，田慧盈
排版設計：健呈電腦排版股份有限公司
錄 音 員：Michael Tennant / Meilee Saccenti / Sara Zittrer / Jacob Roth

董 事 長：洪祺祥
法律顧問：建大法律事務所
財務顧問：高威會計師事務所

出　　版：日月文化出版股份有限公司
製　　作：EZ 叢書館
地　　址：台北市大安區信義路三段 151 號 9 樓
電　　話：(02) 2708-5509
傳　　真：(02) 2708-6157
網　　址：www.ezbooks.com.tw
客服信箱：service@heliopoli.com.tw

總 經 銷：高見文化行銷股份有限公司
電　　話：(02)2668-9005
傳　　真：(02)2668-6220
印　　刷：禹利電子分色有限公司
初　　版：2011 年 11 月
定　　價：250 元
I S B N：978-986-248-214-8